Melanie Martin Goes Dutch

The Private Diary of My Almost Bummer Summer with Cecily, Matt the Brat, and Vincent van Go Go Go

D0964079

OTHER DELL YEARLING BOOKS YOU WILL ENJOY

THE DIARY OF MELANIE MARTIN, *Carol Weston*

A NECKLACE OF RAINDROPS, *Joan Aiken*

TRIA AND THE GREAT STAR RESCUE, *Rebecca Kraft Rector*

AKIKO AND THE INTERGALACTIC ZOO, *Mark Crilley*

HALFWAY TO THE SKY, *Kimberly Brubaker Bradley*

TYLER ON PRIME TIME, *Steve Atinsky*

THE VICTORY GARDEN, *Lee Kochenderfer*

ALL THE WAY HOME, *Patricia Reilly Giff*

GROVER G. GRAHAM AND ME, *Mary Quattlebaum*

SOME KIND OF PRIDE, *Maria Testa*

Melanie Martin Goes Dutch

The Private Diary of My Almost Bummer Summer with Cecily, Matt the Brat, and Vincent van Go Go Go

BY

CAROL WESTON

A DELL YEARLING BOOK

To my niece and nephews
—in order of appearance—
Sarah, Robbie, David, Felix, Jack, and Jules

Published by
Dell Yearling
an imprint of
Random House Children's Books
a division of Random House, Inc.
New York

Visit us on the Web! www.randomhouse.com/kids

Educators and librarians, for a variety of teaching tools, visit us at
www.randomhouse.com/teachers

ISBN: 0-440-41899-2

Reprinted by arrangement with Alfred A. Knopf

Printed in the United States of America

June 2003

10 9 8 7 6 5 4 3 2 1

OPM

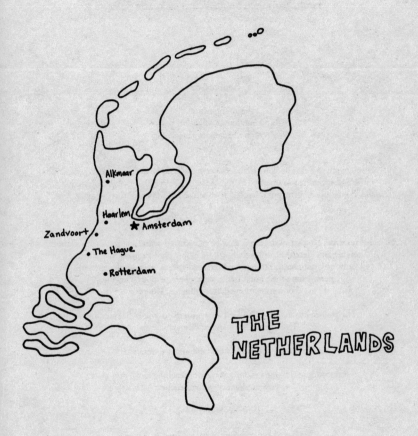

Alkmaar

Haarlem

Zandvoort

★ Amsterdam

The Hague

Rotterdam

THE
NETHERLANDS

$$\newcommand{}{}$$

☾ June 15
🛏 bedtime

Dear Brand New Diary,

I can't believe it!

This was the best day EVER!

School is out, and I, Melanie Martin, am almost a fifth grader.

5ᵗʰ grade!!!

Today at the end-of-fourth-grade party, everybody said my cupcakes were delicious—even Christopher.

Yesterday after we baked, Mom helped me hide them on top of the refrigerator so Dad wouldn't accidentally eat any. Why? Because last time I made cupcakes, Dad gobbled one up without asking permission—and I ended up with twenty cupcakes for twenty-one kids. The next day on the walk to school,

1

I was balancing my cupcake tray and hoping hoping hoping someone would be absent.

Trust me. It does *not* make you feel proud of yourself to be hoping that someone in your class is stuck at home sneezing or barfing. It makes you feel like a bad person. But when you don't have enough cupcakes to go around, everybody except you gets a cupcake, and you have to sit at your desk pretending you didn't want one anyway.

I am *not* that good a person!

Anyway, today was perfect. I brought in the right number of cupcakes, the party was fun, and even Miss Sands was in a great mood. Plus, it was a half day, so we got out at 12:00 instead of 3:00! And almost no homework until September!! YAY!!

(I wrote "almost" because we have to read "at least one long book" and write "at least a hundred words" about what we learned from it.)

The best thing about vacation is that Cecily and I can spend every minute together and have a ton of sleepovers. And not just on weekends!

Mom loves summer vacation too. She just started a five hundred–piece puzzle of a painting of sunflowers. She says puzzles are her "summertime relaxation."

She also says that the only thing she loves more than teaching is vacationing. She says it's much easier to keep track of two kids than a whole class.

I wonder if that's true.

After all, one of her kids *is* Matt the Brat.

4-EVER yours

Melanie Martin, Almost Fifth Grader

June 22

afternoon on the sofa

Dear Diary,

Is this going to be a bummer summer?

School has been out for only a week, and—even though I would never admit this to *anybody*—I sort of miss it. I don't mean waking up early or doing homework or Miss Sands. I mean lunch, recess, art, music, P.E., library, and my friends.

Cecily hasn't been around at all. She's been with her dad. She sent me a postcard from Washington, D.C.

I wish my family would go somewhere.

I wish Cecily would come back.

At home, it's just me and Matt the Brat.

Of all the brothers in the world, I can't believe mine is Matt. When baby boys were being given out, Mom and Dad obviously got in the wrong line. (I think they got into the reptile line.)

To be perfectly honest, Matt and I were actually starting to get along this spring. But then he got seriously annoying again.

He loves to play games. He has ever since he was two. Maybe even before that. He used to sit in his diaper and play "How big is Maaaaaaatt?" "Sooooooo big!" all day long with a dopey two-tooth smile on his face.

Now all he ever wants to do is play Clue Jr. He *lives* to shout, "Mortimer Mustard hid the bird in the bank!" or "Polly Peacock hid the turtle in the wig shop!"

It gets old.

Or maybe *I'm* getting old for junior games.

Last night I mumbled to Dad that I was bored.

4

"Bored?!" Dad said with absolutely no sympathy. "I can think of plenty of things for you to do." So he made me put away dishes and alphabetize his CDs and do a million trillion chores.

Chores chores chores! I was going to accuse him of child abuse, but he would have rolled his eyes and said, "Melanie, pleeeease!"

Once, I did say, "Child abuse! Child abuse!" on the subway and Dad got mad and said it's no joke and what if police officers had taken me seriously? He said I should appreciate the parents I have.

Personally, I think my parents should appreciate me—and understand that I need to be with kids my own age.

My own age: ten and a half. Not Matt's age: six and a half.

Later,

Melanie the Misunderstood

morning in Dad's BIG soft chair

Dear Diary,

Cecily gets back today!

I just called her but I wish I hadn't. When I said, "Is Cecily there?" instead of saying a simple "No," Cecily's mom said, "Melanie, it's more polite to say, 'Hello, Mrs. Hausner, this is Melanie. May I please speak to Cecily?'"

I mumbled, "Okay." But I felt like saying, "I wasn't calling to get a manners lesson. I was calling to talk to my best friend."

Cecily's mom is usually pretty nice. I like when she invites me for dinner or to a movie. And I like that she always has big bags of marshmallows and little bags of M&M's just for us. And I like that last week she helped us have a book sale on Broadway and we both made fifteen dollars.

I *don't* like that she's strict about making us take off our shoes and hang up our sweaters. I also don't like that I have to call her Mrs. Hausner when Cecily gets to call my mom Miranda. (Not that Cecily ever does. She never really calls her anything.)

Anyway, right now I am *trying* to write, but Matt found some of that plastic bubbly wrap that Mom uses for delicate objects and he put it on the floor and started driving all over it on his scooter. He says he's not stopping until he has popped every last bubble.

It sounds like firecrackers.

Matt also has tongue twisters on the brain. He made me say "unique New York, unique New York, unique New York" over and over, so I told him to say "I'm a silly little idiot" five times fast. Then I said, "Matt, if you want to be annoying, go into your room."

He said, "It's no fun being annoying by myself."

Yours with a Sigh ——
Mel

afternoon in the Kitchen

Dear Diary,

I went to Cecily's apartment today and her cat sat on my lap and purred for about an hour. Cecily is lucky she has a cat and a bunny. All we ever have is fish, and half the time they die right away. Like Fluffy and Muffy. And Potato and Chip. And Goldy and Lox. And Wishy and Fishy.

Right now we don't have any pets at all (unless you count Matt).

Cecily's cat is named Cheshire and he always always always purrs. Her bunny is named Honey (short for Honey Bunny) and sometimes she's sweet but sometimes she bites. If you startle her, she actually growls! I think she is part bunny, part tiger.

Today Mrs. Hausner handed us two carrots and we ate two bites each, then gave them to Honey Bunny. We thought that was pretty smart. But later Mrs. Hausner saw the nibbled-on carrot remains in Honey Bunny's cage and said, "I didn't peel those carrots for the rabbit!"

We apologized and went back to drawing pencil portraits of each other (Cecily's a good artist). Then we shut our eyes tight and walked around with our hands in front of us. It's a game called No Peeking. We walked out of Cecily's bedroom, down her hallway, and into her kitchen, where we felt around until we located a big squishy bag of marshmallows. We opened our eyes, opened the bag, opened the microwave, and puffed up the marshmallows one at a time for thirty seconds (no more or they explode).

It was really fun until Cecily's mom started acting crabby again. She asked if we wanted chocolate milk, and I said, "Yes," and she said, "Yes, *please*." Then I was telling a story and I said, "Oh my God!" and she said, "Oh my *gosh!*" She even said that I say "like" and "you know" too much, which made me want to tell her that she is correcting me too much. Like, you know???

She never used to criticize me. Why start now? Doesn't she know my own parents already work overtime on that job?

Well, Cecily and I baked oatmeal cookies, and Mrs.

Hausner took the bowl away *right* when we were about to eat the leftover dough. Then she said that the kitchen looked like a tornado had blown through. I should have kept my mouth shut (duh!), but I said, "It's not thaaaat bad."

She said, "Girls, I'm coming back in five minutes, and I expect this kitchen to look the way it did when you found it."

Cecily and I quietly wiped the countertops, scrubbed the cookie sheets, and ate three warm soft cookies each. Then I got ready to go. I was putting on my shoes at the front door, where Mrs. Hausner makes us leave them, when I made a decision. I decided I'm not going to call and say "Is Cecily there?" or "Hello, Mrs. Hausner, this is Melanie. May I please speak to Cecily?" I decided I'm not going to call at all.

I'm going to let Cecily call me.

So there.

Melanie

Dear Diary,

Cecily didn't call all day.

Mom and I started a new puzzle. It's of purple irises.

XO

M. M.

🛏 bedtime

Dear Diary,

Cecily didn't call tonight either. I wrote this poem:

> It's true that with Cecily,
> I baked sort of messily.
> But rather than criticize,
> Mrs. Hausner should realize
> That when you make something delicious,
> You always get some dirty dishes!

Yours truly,

Melanie Martin,

Cookie Baker

Dear Diary,

Dad let me help paint the window frame in the bathroom. It was fun but hard because he didn't want any brush strokes to show. He wouldn't even *let* Matt help.

The paint we used was called "matte," which Dad said means dull, not bright (hee hee). It was white Dutch Boy paint and the can had a boy on it wearing wooden shoes. Dad said Dutch chemists figured out how to make really great paint way back in the 1500s.

Well, I've been trying to figure out why Cecily hasn't called (or if her mom is mad at me), so I said, "Dad, do you think Cecily is dumping me?"

"Don't be silly. She's probably away," Dad said. "Don't worry so much."

I told him I can't help worrying.

He said, "Mellie, you two have been friends for years. That's not about to change. Now relax. It's not good to be a worrywart."

Can you believe that?

A father calling his daughter a wart?

Wartily yours,

melancholy melanie

June 30

late morning IN mY Room

Dear Diary,

I do NOT get why Cecily hasn't called.

Is she at her father's and forgot to tell me?

Is something wrong?

When she and I became friends back in kinder-garten, we used to love to give our Barbies baths. We had lots of Barbies, and we'd give them all baths, one by one, in the bathroom sink. It took hours. We even shampooed their hair with squirts of toothpaste, which is pretty gross now that I think about it.

Once when we were bathing our Barbies at her apartment, Cecily was quiet the whole entire time. Then, when we were down to the *very last* Barbie, she blurted out, "My mom and dad are getting a divorce." She had barely said a word all day, then suddenly she

13

said *that*. I didn't know what to say, so I think I said something really dumb like "No, they're not," when obviously they were.

And they did.

I wish Cecily would call.
I do not like this at all.

Lonelily,
Mel

P.S. If lonelily is not a word, it should be.

July 1
noon

Dear Diary,

I am So So So embarrassed!

I called three times this morning. Each time Cecily's mom answered, and since I didn't feel like saying "Hello, Mrs. Hausner, this is Melanie. May I please speak to Cecily?" I hung up. The third time, before I could put the phone down, Cecily's mom said, "For

14

heaven's sake, Melanie, don't keep hanging up on me. We have Caller I.D., so I know it's you and—"

I felt sooooo stupid that instead of apologizing like a mature human being, I did something even stupider: I hung up again!

God, I'm an idiot. (I mean, *gosh*, I'm an idiot.)

Idiotically yours,

Melanie the Moron

P.S. Why didn't Cecily tell me they got Caller I.D.?

July 2

In the Kitchen after lunch

Dear Diary,

The phone rang and I was hoping it was Cecily, but Mom answered and after the call, she stuck her arms straight up in the air as if she'd won a marathon.

"I got the grant!" she said.

"What's a grant?" I asked.

She said a grant is when someone gives you money to study something. She said she has asked for grants

15

before but has never gotten one, and now she was just awarded a small one to study van Gogh.

"The guy who chopped his ear off?" Matt asked. Mom's always talking about artists, so Matt and I know who's who.

"Yes," Mom said. "He's also 'the guy' who painted the flowers on the puzzles we've been doing. Oh, I am so happy! We're going to the Van Gogh Museum!"

"Today?" I asked. I'd never heard of it, so it's not like I've been dying to go or anything.

"Not today," Mom said. "It's in Amsterdam."

Mom looked completely happy and Matt looked completely confused.

"In Holland," I explained. In third grade we learned that, hundreds of years ago, Dutch people had sailed from Amsterdam to a place they named *New* Amsterdam. Later it got renamed . . . New York!

Matt asked, "Where's Holland?"

Mom said, "In Europe."

"Europe," Matt repeated. "That's a funny word."

"No, it's not," I said. "It sounds like 'syrup' or 'You're up!'"

"Or 'Throw up!'" Matt said.

"Or 'Grow up!' and 'Shut up!'" I added. I thought that was pretty funny, but I could tell Mom didn't, so I asked when we were going.

"Next month," she said. "During Daddy's vacation week. It's good our passports are up to date."

Our passports are up to date because of our trip to Italy this spring. Kids' passports last five years—which means I'm practically permanently stuck with my squinty, dorky passport photo.

Mom says grown-ups' passports last ten years because grown-ups don't change as fast as kids. Grown-ups are already grown up. Even if they get grayer or balder or fatter or shorter, you can still recognize them.

Well, Matt started getting as excited as Mom, and next thing you know, he was hopping around like a bouncing bunny. What a weirdo. I'm surprised our neighbors in the apartment downstairs didn't complain.

Mom called Dad at work and said, "Can you believe I got it?" He must have known all about the grant because Mom didn't have to say what "it" was or anything. After she hung up, she put a bottle of champagne in the fridge.

By then, Matt wasn't just hopping, he was also singing—and *swearing*—at the top of his lungs. He was saying, "Amster Amster Dam Dam Dam!"

And get this: Mom was letting him get away with it!

LUV,
mellie

P.S. I'm dying to call Cecily, but I keep thinking she'll call me. I'm also tempted to tell Mom about Cecily's mom, but she'd probably take Mrs. Hausner's side. And I could never admit that I hung up on her three times!

bedtime

Dear Diary,

Dad came home from work with a big package. For a second I was hoping he had brought Matt and me a present for no reason (not that he ever has). But he handed it right to Mom.

Off came the wrapping paper and out came a bunch of tulips.

It was a little disappointing.

Not for Mom, though. She loves tulips. She kissed Dad right on the lips and said, "Aren't these the prettiest things you've ever seen?"

"No," Matt said. He probably thinks Lily upstairs is the prettiest thing he's ever seen. They've been in love since they were born. Last week they wrote their names in big dark purple letters on the sidewalk. They wrote Matt + Lily using mulberries from the tree outside our building. The letters have faded to a light brown, but you can still read them.

Anyway, the tulips are really fancy. When Mom buys tulips at the corner grocer, she gets the cheap kind that looks like green sticks with Easter eggs on top. She buys them all January and February because she says they remind her that spring (and spring break) is coming.

Dad's tulips bend and curve gracefully, and their petals look like frilly, colorful feathers, all lacy around the edges.

He said he had to go to a special florist to get them.

"What came over you?" Mom asked.

"Holland is the tulip capital of the world," Dad

said. Mom looked puzzled, so Dad admitted, "It was Helen's idea." Helen is Dad's assistant.

"I should have guessed," Mom said, but she didn't seem to mind.

Mom arranged the tulips in a vase, one at a time, and told Matt and me to go get our art kits. Vacation or not, Mom can't help being an art teacher.

Next thing you know, I heard a POP and Mom and Dad were drinking champagne and talking about frequent-flier miles, and Matt and I were drinking ginger ale and drawing tulips.

Matt, by the way, is a horrible artist.

Mom used to look at his pictures and say things like, "I love the colors you chose! Tell me about this." Well, trust me. "Tell me about this" is art-teacher language for "I have no clue what this big messy blob is. A car? A dog? Give me a hint!"

Matt never even got offended. He'd just patiently explain his pathetic picture to her. "Here's the dinosaur and here's the rocket ship and here's the moon and here's the sun."

And you know what? Mom never said, "There were no rocket ships in dinosaur days!" or "You can't stick the moon next to the sun!" Never. Not once. Mom said, "The moon next to the sun! Oh Matt, that's soooo creative!"

Matt still stinks at drawing, but at least now you can tell what he's trying to draw. It's not a *total* guessing game.

Me, I'm an excellent artist, if I do say so myself. I think I'm as good as Cecily.

Mom thinks I should always carry a sketch pad. I like carrying a diary instead.

Anyway, we sketched and sketched and colored and colored, and then Mom put our work up in the Gallery. That's what she calls the doors of our coat closet.

"These pictures are beautiful," she said.

I thought mine was and Matt's wasn't, but I didn't say anything. Now that they're hanging side by side, it's pretty obvious whose is better.

Tonight Mom came to tuck me in and said she loved my drawing.

"I bet you said the same exact thing to Matt," I said. Mom smiled, so I asked, "Do you love me more than Matt?"

I ask her that a lot. I don't know why because the question annoys her and she never says yes.

Tonight, though, she was in such a good mood, she didn't get annoyed. She just kissed me and said, "I love you both with all my heart."

She was about to leave, but I said, "You took a long time with Matt. Take a long time with me."

So Mom sort of stroked my hair and said she thinks we're going to have a wonderful time in Holland. Then she said, "You can write a little more, but don't stay up too late, okay?"

I said I wouldn't. And see? I didn't.

night-night!

Melanie the Artist.

July 3

morning

Dear Diary,

Mom gave me *Anne Frank: The Diary of a Young Girl.* It was the copy that she had when she was a teenager. She said that I could read it alone or she could read it to me or both. I picked both.

Mom said Anne's story is very sad and very important

and that she'll explain it to me as we go along. Anne was a girl who had to hide during World War II to save her life. We will visit the place in Holland where she hid with her family.

Today we read just a few pages. Anne Frank started her diary on her thirteenth birthday (well, two days after) and she wrote, "I want to write, but more than that, I want to bring out all kinds of things that lie buried deep in my heart."

Diaries are good for that.

Friends are too.

Happy Almost Independence Day,

Mel

Dear Diary, night

Matt asked, "What color M&M's do you like best?"

I said, "Brown, then red, then yellow, in that order."

"I like blue."

"I hate blue!"

"Why?"

"Because food should not be blue, except for blue-berries."

"Blue is my *favorite* food color! Blue cotton candy and blue jelly beans and blue ice pops."

"Yeah, well, you're a doo-doo head." (That sort of slipped out.)

"Well, you're an E.B.S." (That means Evil Big Sister.)

"Only because you're an A.L.B." (That means Annoying Little Brother.)

"Hey, Melanie, how come Cecily hasn't been over?" Matt asked. "Are you guys in a fight?"

Out loud I said, "No."

But inside, I started to feel . . . blue blue blue.

Bluely yours,

M&M Mel

July 4
almost 6:00

Dear Diary,

No wonder Cecily hadn't called me back!

I just found out what's going on.

Cecily finally called and Matt and I both picked

up the phone. Matt pretended to hang up, but I could tell he hadn't because I could hear him breathing in and out. "Hang up N-O-W!" I yelled, and he did. (Even Matt knows what N-O-W spells.)

Cecily said she was sorry she hadn't called, but she and her mom have been going to doctors' appointments, and she didn't want to talk yet because she had some scary news that she kept hoping would change.

"*What?*" I asked. That's when Cecily told me that her mother has a disease. She got a test and they found out she has breast cancer and she might have to have an operation.

I'm glad Cecily called but I feel terrible for her and her mom.

Breast cancer! I've heard of it, but I've never known anybody who had it.

Now I feel kind of guilty that I wrote that Mrs. Hausner has been acting crabby. I mean, she's obviously been stressed and stuff! I wonder how bad it is. I wonder if she looks different.

This sounds really stupid, but tonight we're going to a Fourth of July picnic in Central Park, and I'm going to try not to look at Cecily's mother's chest. It's not like I normally do or anything. But I'm afraid I might accidentally glance at her chest and I wouldn't want Cecily or her mom to catch me doing that.

Once, I was reading the front of a lady's T-shirt because it had all these jokes on it. But then the lady stared at me staring at her. She thought *I* was a perv when *she* was the one with jokes all over her chest.

I hope Cecily's mom will be okay!!

I asked Cecily if she'd mind if I told my mom about her mom and she said no. She said her mom is on the phone all the time now with doctors and friends.

concerned,
mel

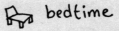 bedtime

Dear Diary,

At the picnic, first there were fireflies; then there were fire*works*! Red, white, and blue ones, like giant sparklers in the sky.

Cecily's mom looks the same as ever. If I didn't know something was wrong, I would never have guessed.

When I saw her, I knew that the first thing I should do was apologize for having hung up on her, and the second was say "Get well soon" or "I hope you feel better." I *knew* I should do that. But somehow all I could squeak out was a pitiful little "Hi, Mrs. Hausner," as though things were normal. She said, "Hi," and acted normal back.

I feel kind of guilty that I didn't do the right thing.

On my first sleepover ever, which was at Cecily's, I got scared and worried. Cecily's mom made me cocoa and told me about *her* first sleepover and how she got scared and worried too. She helped me feel better.

Being homesick and being sick-sick aren't the same, but still, I wish I had thought of something nice to say.

Well, Cecily and I climbed a tree so we could spy on everyone. She told me some more about the scary news. She said her mom had felt a little surprise lump in her chest.

"Like a pebble?" I asked.

"More like a pencil eraser, I think," Cecily said.

Cecily's mom got it x-rayed, then another doctor

gave her a needle test. He said she has cancer, so now she's asking a different doctor for a second opinion. But she will probably have to have an operation. Cecily says cancer is when bad cells in your body multiply and have to be cut out or poisoned with chemicals or both.

While Cecily was talking to me, Cecily's mom was talking to my parents. Cecily and I usually talk a lot, but our parents usually don't.

We all left the picnic together. Cecily's mom kept stopping to throw away empty bottles that other people had littered. Mrs. Hausner is a big cleaner-upper. She loves Central Park and she hates trash.

After we said goodbye, I asked my mom, "Is she going to be okay?" Mom said she thinks so and Dad told me not to worry.

worried anyway,
mel

July 11
morning

Dear Diary,

    We fly to Europe on August 11. That's in exactly
O N E month!!!

      EXCITED——

      Mellie

July 13
bedtime

Dear Diary,

    Cecily came over and Mom took us to Riverside Park,
and Matt made us play Who Can Spit Watermelon Seeds
the Farthest. Matt is good at it and Cecily is great at it and
I stink at it. I don't know why I can't do it. Even when I
concentrate and curl my tongue and spit them up and
out, the seeds still land just a foot away.

    Mom asked Cecily how her mom is doing. Cecily
said, "Okay, I guess."

    Mom put her arm around her.

    Kind of sadly,

    Mel

on the sofa after dinner

Dear Diary,

You will never ever believe this!

It is too good to be true!

Guess who is going with us to Amster Amster Dam Dam Dam?

Cecily!

Cecily's mom scheduled her operation for when we would be away, because Mom said that while it might be hard for her to take care of Cecily during all the hospital stuff, it would be easy for our family to take care of her and we'd love to—in Holland! Mom got the idea when we were spitting out watermelon seeds, but Cecily's parents had to talk on the phone about it. Now they're buying Cecily a plane ticket!

Instead of a family of four, we'll be a family of five!

Cecily and I will be sisters!

I'm so HaPPY!

Happy Happy HAPPY!

At dinner Matt said, "It's not fair that Melanie gets to take a friend and I don't."

He sort of had a point, so I just stared quietly at my meatballs.

"Matt, Cecily's mom is sick," Mom said.

"If Lily's mom got sick, could Lily come with us?" Matt asked. He was eating his spaghetti in a really disgusting way. He doesn't twirl it, he loads up his mouth and then bites off all the extra noodles. He always looks like a mama bird with a beak stuffed with worms.

"Matt," Mom said, "let's be glad Lily's mom is *not* sick. We're taking Cecily along because it will help her mom, and it won't be that hard for us."

"That's what you think," Matt said. "You have Dad, and Mel has Cecily, and I'll probably get lost again. Remember the Sixteen Chapel?"

"The *Sistine* Chapel," Dad corrected, then added, "This time we'll stick together." (It was pretty bad when Matt got lost on our last trip.)

Anyway, I just kept minding my own business, watching my meatballs. I have to admit, though, I'd probably be mad if Matt got to take someone and I didn't.

Oh well! That's the way the meatball bounces!

The rest of dinner was a big fat lecture from Dad about how we are privileged children and how we should appreciate our health and good fortune and not take it for granted and not get spoiled, etc. etc. etc.

We promised we'd try.

When Dad was done lecturing, Mom started in about table manners and how Matt should twirl his spaghetti or at least take smaller bites—like Melanie (hee hee).

Your privileged friend,

MELLER ° ° O

P.S. That's one of Dad's nicknames for me.
P.P.S. Three weeks until Holland!

July 22
bedtime

Dear Diary,

Matt got hurt today. It was really scary. We were playing softball in the park. Matt was catcher and I was pitcher and the second grader who lives across the street was batter and his baby-sitter was keeping an eye on all of us. Well, the second grader kept taking practice swings and I guess Matt must have been standing too close to him because suddenly the bat bonked Matt *right in the nose*. He started to *wail*.

At first I thought Matt's nose had gone flying off or something! Blood was gushing all down his face. None of us knew whether his nose was broken or his teeth were bashed in or what.

The baby-sitter took us right home. Matt was crying and bleeding, but by then at least I could tell that his nose was still on his face and his teeth were still in his mouth.

It turned out that he got hurt right *between* his nostrils. That little piece of skin that sort of holds noses down got ripped.

Fortunately, Mom was home. She cleaned Matt up and stuck big cotton balls in his nostrils. (I have to say, he looked pretty weird.) Then she called the doctor, and next thing you know, all three of us were in a taxi.

Matt said, "I can't breathe. Am I going to die?"

Mom said, "No, sweetie! You'll be fine. Just breathe through your mouth," and cuddled him extra close.

Matt looked relieved. It was as if mouth breathing had never occurred to him.

The doctor sewed in three stitches (Matt's first) and said Matt would have swelling and bruises but he'd be fine.

When we got back home, Dad was already there. He even had a stuffed animal—a walrus—for Matt.

Dad never gives me anything unless it's my birthday.

Since you're my diary and I can tell you anything, I have a terrible awful confession. At first I was all worried about Matt, but now I'm already getting sick of hearing him tell everyone on the phone about his life-or-death accident.

When I hurt my eyebrow, my family didn't make this much fuss.

Not one friend or relative telephoned. (We were in Italy, but *still*.)

And I got *seven* stitches. Not three.

I should probably not think like this, right?

Well, maybe I'm not as good a person as I should be.

I mean, *most* of me is very nice.

But maybe a tiny speck of me is not so nice.

Or maybe a small chunk?

I can't believe I'm admitting this. Even to you.

Honestly yours,
Melanie

July 26
In the Kitchen

Dear Diary,

Cecily and I were playing with her Magic 8 Ball. It tells fortunes. We like to ask it questions like "Will I be famous when I grow up?" or "Will there be a lot of homework in fifth grade?" or "Will I marry Christopher?" It gives answers like "Cannot Predict Now" or "Outlook Good" or "Don't Count on It."

I was thinking of asking "Am I a good enough person?" but I didn't want to say that out loud. Since Cecily hadn't said anything about her mother, I asked if she wanted to ask about her mom.

"I don't even want to do this anymore," Cecily

said. She put the 8 Ball back on her shelf under her collage of magazine celebrities. Then she started brushing her hair and looking at herself in her mirror.

I looked too, and her reflection sort of caught me by surprise. Cecily has gotten taller. And prettier. She's even developing a little.

I'm still the exact same as always. I think.

Anyway, I can't believe my family is about to temporarily adopt my BFF—Best Friend Forever!

Going to Amsterdam will be great.
Cecily and I can hardly wait!

Love and Kisses,
Melleroonie—(another nickname)

P.S. Matt's face is still greenish-bluish-purplish, but the bruises are fading. At the grocery store, the cashier joked, "Did you slug your little brother?" I answered, "No, but sometimes I feel like it!" She laughed laughed laughed, but Mom looked unamused.

at my desk at ☼ dusk

Dear Diary,

I just beat Dad at Hangman. I hanged him with the word "phlegm." I almost hanged him with the word "diarrhea."

I can't believe I hanged Dad! He didn't mind, though. I think he was impressed. He said my vocabulary was expanding. He didn't know I knew that phlegm is the gross stuff people cough up.

Speaking of disgusting substances (like phlegm and diarrhea), yesterday Matt stepped in dog doo and today a bird pooped on his arm. A runny little white-and-black poop landed right on him! Yuck! (And hee hee!)

I never knew my little brother was a doo-doo magnet!

Matt washed his arm the *second* he got home. He said it wasn't fair because everyone knows you're supposed to check the ground for dog doo, but no one ever says you're supposed to check the air for bird doo. He said he was mad at that bird.

"It's not like it pooped on you deliberately," I said.

He asked what deliberately meant.

38

I said, "On purpose," and then I wrote a poem.

Matt got pooped on by a bird.
While he washed away the turd,
I taught him a brand new word.

English is tricky. Bird, turd, and word all rhyme even though they have different vowels. Isn't that the weirdest thing you ever *heard*? (And isn't Matt a little *nerd*?)

Creatively yours,

Melanie of the Expanding Vocabulary

P.S. Matt's stitches are out and his face is back to normal (if you can call Matt's face normal).

August 1

Morning in the kitchen

Dear Diary,

We're going bowling. YAY! Dad said that bowling goes back to ancient times and that Dutch settlers

39

introduced it to America. It used to be called ninepins because it had (duh) nine pins. But some people started betting on who would win and so ninepins got outlawed. Well, guess what? The people added a pin and started playing *tenpins* because tenpins was *not* illegal!

Guess what else? Dad and Mom now consider bowling an educational activity. Works for me!

A perfect game is twelve strikes XXXXXXXXXXXX. I'd be thrilled with just one strike X or two strikes XX.

XX (Get it?),

Melanie who never gets a str◯ke ●

P.S. Holland Countdown: Ten Days Till Takeoff!

August 5
bedtime

Dear Diary,

Mom and I have been reading Anne Frank's diary. Anne always starts out "Dear Kitty" and usually ends with "Yours, Anne."

I wonder if I should name you.

Anne Frank was really brave. Here's what happened. Adolf Hitler was the leader of Germany and he was not just a bad person, he was *evil*. Like a monster. And crazy! He wanted everyone to be blond when even he wasn't blond. Well, he hated Jews (which made no sense) and he got the Germans to take over Amsterdam and kick Jewish people *out of their homes* and send them away to terrible places called concentration camps!

Instead of waiting to be caught and sent away, Anne's family decided to "disappear"—to go into hiding until World War II was over.

But since Jews no longer had the freedom to go wherever they wanted, the Franks couldn't just load up their suitcases and leave. So you know what they did? They put on "heaps of clothes"—pants, vests, jackets, coats, probably even underwear—and waddled out dressed as if they were going to "the North Pole" (that's how Anne put it). Anne also packed a small bag and the first thing she put in it was her diary.

I would have done that too.

Well, they all hurried into their hiding place, which was the attic apartment above the office of

Anne's father, Otto Frank. It became their new home. At first, Anne was scared, but she wrote that it didn't feel like hiding—"more like being on vacation in a very peculiar boarding house."

No one knew they were there except the friends who snuck them in and brought them food. No one else could know—not even all the people who cleaned or worked in the office right beneath them.

It's hard to imagine having to stay in a hiding place for years. I mean, it wasn't a game of hide-and-seek. If you got found, you would be *taken away*. During the day, the Franks could not even look out the window, and when people were working downstairs, they could not run water or cough or stomp around or make any noise at all. Even at night they couldn't make much noise, but at least they could flush the toilet and listen to the radio if they kept the volume down.

But they could never go out. Not even to see a doctor. Not even to see a friend.

Yours,
Melanie

Dear Diary,

I know Anne called her diary "Kitty" but I can't think of a good name for you, so I'm going to stick with "Diary."

<u>TOMORROW</u> we leave so I wrote another poem.

*We're about to say hello
To tulips and van Gogh!*

I've been packing my favorite clothes. I'll also pack my art kit and cards and Anne Frank's diary and you—my diary—right in my backpack. That way, I'll have something to do for seven hours if Cecily conks out on the plane.

Tomorrow I'll pack Hedgehog. She's so small and soft that I *could* squoosh her in my backpack, but what if I forget her at the airport or on the plane? Instead, I'll pack her with the clothes in Matt's and my bag so she'll be snug and safe until we get there.

Guess what? We ordered in Chinese food and Matt's and my fortune cookie fortunes were both about going away! I am taping them in here.

Matt's:

> You are about to embark on a most delightful journey.

Mine:

> Sometimes travel to new places leads to great transformation.

Dad expanded my vocabulary by explaining that "transformation" means change.

Fortunately yours (Get it?),

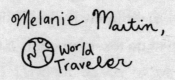
Melanie Martin,
World Traveler

Dear Diary,

I'm waiting to board.

I'm bored of waiting!

When you fly to a different country, you're supposed to get to the airport very very early.

Thanks to me, we did. That's because I recited my latest poem:

C'mon, let's go!
We're in a hurry!
Let's grab a cab—
Or I will worry!

We are now at the gate.

Cecily and I took a magazine quiz called "How Well Do You Know Your Best Friend?" It had questions like "Who is your best friend's crush?" (we both wrote Christopher) and "How many children will she have someday?" (we both wrote two) and "What does your BFF want to be when she grows up?" (Cecily wrote "writer" for me; I wrote "actress" for her).

The scoring section said that we were "Totally Tight"—which, duh, we already knew!

Dad bought himself a New Amsterdam beer (he thought that was pretty clever) and bought us small bags of potato chips. Matt got barbecue, and Cecily and I got plain because we both hate barbecue and both love plain.

It's fun traveling with someone who likes the same exact stuff I do!

Uh-oh. Time to, as the airline people put it, "board the aircraft." Gotta go.

g^2g,

Melanie in America

Dear Diary,
on board

When you get on a plane, it is not very ideal that regular passengers have to walk right by first-class passengers. They have big, cozy, comfortable seats and stretched-out legs, and they get snacks and drinks right away, while regular people (like us) are all smooshed in the back, hungry and thirsty.

Personally, I don't like having to walk by first-class passengers. I doubt they're saying "Nyaaa-nyaaa nya nyaaa-nyaaaaaa" or anything, but they probably think they're cool and we're not.

I mentioned this to Dad and he said that when I grow up, I can make tons of money and do whatever I want, but right now I'm lucky to be flying around at all. He said that at my age, he didn't even have a passport, let alone go skittering off to Europe with a best friend at a moment's notice.

Well, excuuuuse me! I was just making an observation. Dad didn't have to sound so annoyed about it.

I told Cecily about walking past first-class passengers and she agreed with me completely.

It's so cooool that she and I are having a sleepover on an airplane!

Mom and Dad said to try to sleep because when we get to Europe, it won't be bedtime—it will be morning, like it or not.

Here's what they don't get: It's hard to sleep when you're excited. And we haven't even had dinner yet.

We just had dinner. I don't know what they ate in first class, but the second-class people had to choose between fish (yuck!) and chicken. Chicken would have been okay except that it came with rice and salad, which might have been okay, except the rice had little corn kernels and bits of green pepper in it, and the salad had slivers of beets in it, and the chicken had no flavor. Not counting my bread and my brownie, I gave most of my dinner to Dad.

Dad eats anything. When it comes to food, he's a total vacuum cleaner. I told Cecily that sometimes we tease him about being a Big Pig (or B.P.), but only when he's in a good mood.

We're in row 17. This is how we're sitting: Mom, Dad, Matt, Cecily, me. There's an aisle between Matt and Cecily. I'm glad I'm not sitting next to Matt because one of his baby teeth is loose and he keeps wiggling it and it's driving me crazy.

It's not driving Cecily crazy. She thinks it's funny.

Matt just got up and said, "Mind if I watch you write in your diarrhea? I mean, diary?"

I told him to get a life. But it reminded me of what I just read in Anne Frank's diary.

The lady the Frank family had to live with, Mrs. Van Daan, said, "Hey, Anne, can't I just have a look?"

"I'm afraid not."

"Just the last page then?"

"No, I'm sorry."

Well, poor Anne was nervous because "there was an unflattering description of her" on that very page!

I wish we were flying nonstop to Amsterdam. We're not because by the time we planned this trip, all the cheap nonstop tickets were sold out. So we're flying to London, then switching planes.

I also wish that my chair were more comfortable. It has a headrest, but I'm not tall enough for my head to rest on it. In fact, the top of my head comes up to the bottom of the headrest. So it's almost as if the headrest is resting on my head, which is not restful.

I do like my blue blanket and white pillow and little writing tray.

So far it has been an excellent flight. Not too many bumps. The pilot said to expect a few, though. When he said that, I made a scared face to Cecily and she said, "Don't worry."

I don't know why, but instead of making me feel better, that made me feel worse. It's not like I worry deliberately.

In front of us, a screen is showing a map with a cartoon picture of our plane halfway between the United States and Europe. Later there will be a movie, but it sounds like it's for grown-ups.

The screen is now showing the time in the airports where we started and where we'll land. It is 11:00 P.M. in New York (late!) and 4:00 A.M. in London (early!). But it's about to be *yesterday* in New York and it's already *tomorrow* in London.

Mom, Dad, and Matt have fallen fast asleep. Dad's head is flopped forward and Matt's mouth is wide open. Cecily is reading her magazine, but her eyes are getting droopy, and she's starting to blink in slow motion.

Behind us, a big lady is snoring like crazy. I wish someone would poke her.

I'm going to try to sleep, but it's not easy to sleep in a chair when it's noisy and you're wearing clothes. Sometimes it's not easy to sleep in a bed when it's quiet and you're wearing pajamas!

Unsleepily yours,
Mellie in Midair

August 12

On an airport bench

nine in the morning in Amsterdam
but middle of the night in New York

Dear Diary,

The airline people lost our luggage! We've been sitting here in this Dutch airport for hours and hours watching baggage go around and around and none of it is ours. Tons of people got *their* luggage. Even the big snoring lady grabbed hers and went on her merry way.

I am so

MAD MAD MAD!!

Here's what happened. Once we got to London, we had to race onto a bus that took us to another bus that took us to a different plane that was going to Amsterdam. Our luggage was supposed to tag along with us, but did it? *Noooooo!*

When we first got here, I could barely keep my eyes open.

Now I'm not even sleepy.

It's hard to be mad and sleepy at the same time.

Mom and Dad had to fill out a bunch of papers called Baggage Claim Forms, which asked what our luggage looked like and whether it contained any "valuables."

"What did you pack?" Dad asked us. "Nothing valuable, right?"

"Valuable?" I said. "I packed Hedgehog! And all my favorite clothes." My voice came out shaky and I was trying not to cry.

"I packed DogDog," Matt said, and he did start to cry. Mom packs for him. He couldn't care less about clothes; he just cares about DogDog.

Poor DogDog has already been lost once, in Italy.

Matt looked so pathetic, I almost felt sorry for him. I was considering putting my arm around him and being a Perfect Big Sister—a P.B.S. But right then *Cecily* gave Matt a big hug and said, "Don't worry." It sort of made me mad that *she* was acting like a P.B.S. And that *she* was telling Matt not to worry about losing DogDog and me not to worry about bumps.

Mom and Dad asked Cecily what she had packed, and she said, "Clothes and a gift for you two, but nothing I need right away, so don't worry."

Wait a sec. Now Cecily is telling my *parents* not to worry???

I'm probably just cranky because I hardly got any sleep.

Well, the luggage people said we should wait for the next flight from London. So we did. Cecily and I started playing my favorite hand game, Quackadilioso. But Matt wanted to play. I said, "You don't even know how." Cecily said, "That's okay. We can teach him." Ten seconds later, the two of *them* were clapping away.

Which was fine. Who wants to clap in public anyway?

I'm just looking around at posters of colorful tulips and pretty windmills and at signs in Dutch and English. No Smoking in Dutch is *Niet Roken* (Neat Row Ken). Beware of Pickpockets is *Let Op Zakkenrollers* (Let Op Zock En Rrrollers).

Zakkenrollers. Isn't that the weirdest word??

I'm also listening to people talking different languages. I can't understand a single syllable.

Mostly I am just trying to take my mind off my worries. But I'm still worried. What if Hedgehog is in Africa or Asia or Antarctica and I never see her again?

Mom says she's between New York and Amsterdam and I should be patient.

I'm trying, but patience has never been my specialty.

Little poems are my specialty.

> I can't help it—I'm in a huff
> I really wish I had my stuff!

Impatiently—

Melanie (but not Hedgehog :-)

Dear Diary,   elevenish

Well, we waited and waited for the next flight from London and when it arrived, we watched tons more happy tourists pick up their luggage. All that did was get us madder and tireder.

More tired.

Whatever.

The luggage people apologized (big of them) and said they will send us our luggage as soon as they locate it.

They better!

What a Big Fat Waste of Time. Instead of getting a lovely first impression of Holland, we spent the whole morning in Schiphol Airport (Mom calls it Ski Pole).

We have now decided to take a taxi to where we're staying even though we won't be able to unpack.

"We're giving up?" I asked.

Mom said sometimes it's wise to give up.

Dad said it's time to begin our vacation.

Matt said his tooth is getting really loose.

Cecily didn't say anything because she is in the *toiletten* (Twa Let Ten). In the *toiletten*, you have two choices: *Dames* (Dom Iss) or *Heren* (Hair Ren). *Heren* starts with Her, which is why I almost almost almost went in the wrong door! Fortunately a nice Dutch man said, "No, no, over there." Later Mom told me that dame is an old-fashioned slang word for woman, like damsel, and that *Dames* is the door to pick if you're a dame.

Your Damsel~in~Distress
Melanie in Europe

Dear Diary,

HELLO HOLLand!!

We are staying in the coooooolest place! It's a canal house, which is a big house next to a canal (*kanaal*, pronounced Con Ahl). That's a man-made river. The house used to be the home of a rich family. We just checked in and we're on the third floor, but there's no elevator, so we came up this dark staircase with steps that were so steep and narrow that Dad had to turn his big feet sideways just to walk up them. We have a suite. Mom and Dad share the bedroom, and Cecily, Matt, and I share the living room. Cecily and I are going to sleep on a big, soft, comfortable sofa bed (yay!) and Matt will sleep on a stiff little cot (hee hee).

I'm glad we have our own room. Sometimes when we take trips, Mom and Dad and Matt and I share one room, and that can start out cozy but end up messy.

Here's what I love about this hotel: When you look out the window, you see water where you expect to see a street. And boats! Big boats, little boats, motorboats, sailboats, even paddleboats. Some boats are actually *parked* along the canal. And some boats are houseboats that people live in all the time. You can see tricycles on them and flapping laundry. People actually have birthday parties on them! We also saw one boat that was in the shape of a wooden shoe!

Matt is standing at the window waving like crazy to all the boat passengers. A few have waved back.

Mom said that in winter, the canals freeze over, and instead of boats, there are skaters out there. She said that in Holland, people sometimes skate from one city to another.

"Awesome!" Matt said.

Dad got out his guidebook and told us to sit down. I sat on one side and Cecily sat on the other, and he showed us where we are on the map. Picture a spiderweb that is blue—as if the web were water—and plunk it on top of a bunch of land, and that is what Amsterdam looks like.

New York's streets and avenues are wide and mostly go straight up and down or side to side. (Manhattan is like a long, skinny waffle that's been nibbled on.) Amsterdam's streets and canals are skinny and mostly curve in half-circles.

"It's sooo cooool," Cecily said. "The canals look like the ripples a stone makes when you throw it in water."

Dad said, "They sort of do, don't they?"

Mom came over. "You're right. They fan out just like ripples."

I was going to say that to me, the canals looked like a big blue spiderweb. I didn't, though.

Okay. I have another awful confession. I'm suddenly

not a hundred percent totally positive that having Cecily along is such a great idea after all.

Matt, Mom, and Dad seem to think it is.

Here is my new poem.

Amsterdam is full of curves.
Cecily's getting on my nerves.

Grumpily yours,
Melanie the NOBODY

on a park bench.

Dear Diary,

Mom and Dad hardly ever let us go to Burger King in New York, but we were all acting so fussy (well, *I* was anyway) that I think they took pity, and believe it or not, the first thing we spent our foreign money on was burgers from Burger King! We ate them right here on benches in a square with pigeons cooing and pecking and strutting all around us.

My burger was good except it had a pickle with ketchup and mustard mixed up on the top bun because

Dad didn't know how to say "plain." Dad also bought French fries, which Matt called Dutch fries and which Dad said Dutch people eat with *mayonnaise*. Cecily and I said, "Ewww!" at the same time, then "Jinx!" at the same time. Then we laughed.

Matt said, "Melanie, are you in a better mood now that you have a booger in your belly?"

Cecily cracked up.

"That's not funny, Matt," I explained. "That is first-grade humor. In a few years, you'll look back and realize what a dork you were."

"Do you look back and think *you* were a dork in first grade?" Matt asked.

"I was never a dork," I answered. "I was always very mature for my age."

Matt has *never* been mature for his age.

Mom and Dad were not paying attention to us or to the pigeons. They were sitting on a bench singing old Beatles songs. Parents can be so embarrassing!

Dad said that when John Lennon and Yoko Ono got married, they honeymooned in a hotel in Amsterdam and had a "bed-in for world peace."

60

Mom looked at Dad and, probably to change the subject to something more appropriate, said how beautiful Amsterdam is. So I looked around. And you know what?

This city
Is pretty!

There are cafés everywhere with sidewalk tables with big umbrellas and lots of people talking and laughing.

And there are tons of canals with little stone bridges over them. The canals are lined with short old houses—no skyscrapers—that sprout right up out of the water. We saw ducks paddling on the canals. And we saw a dog scamper out of a canal and shake shake shake water drops from its back.

Mom said, "Amsterdam is sometimes called the Venice of the North," and told us that Venice, in Italy, is famous for its beautiful canals.

Here's the problem: Mom and Dad are on one bench, Cecily and Matt are on another, and I am by myself.

On the outside, I may look normal.

On the inside, I feel left out.

Well, even though I feel alone, I am not alone. I just dropped my smeary top bun and I am having a major pigeon party.

Yours from Pigeon Central,

Inside-Out
Mel

bedtime at the Canal house

Dear Diary,

Bicycles, bicycles, bicycles. Amsterdam is full of bicycles. People get around by boat, car, bus, tram, and foot, but mostly *bicycle*. Streets don't just have sidewalks next to them; they have bike lanes! Everywhere you hear the ting-ting of bicycle bells because ringing the little bells is how bicyclists say "Watch out" to each other.

It's very cool!!

We saw men and women all dressed up for work bicycling with briefcases in their baskets. And we saw people bicycling with dogs on leashes running beside them. We even saw enormous *bicycle parking lots* full of hundreds and hundreds of bikes, some shiny but most rusty. Dad said that in Holland, almost every single person owns a bicycle.

We decided to go bicycling too, so after lunch, we rented four bicycles (Matt is too little to get his own—ha ha). The bikes we rented didn't have fancy gears. They were old black ones with foot brakes. Dad tied a folded-up newspaper to the flat metal part behind his seat so it would be more comfortable for Matt's squooshy tushy.

Amsterdam is crowded, which is bad for biking. But it is also flat, which is great for biking. (I don't like hills for two reasons: I get tired going up them and scared going down them.)

Well, I can't imagine us all biking together in Manhattan, but off we went! Dad led the way with Matt hanging on for dear life, Cecily next, me after that, and Mom last. Mom's job was to make sure none of us fell and cracked our heads open. She said we should have brought helmets since people here don't seem to rent them or use them. Dad said that even if we had brought helmets, they'd be inside our lost luggage, so they wouldn't do us any good.

"I still wish you kids had helmets," Mom said.

"We'll be careful," Cecily said. "Don't worry."

Why does it bug me every time Cecily tells someone not to worry?

To tell you the truth, when we were bicycling, I couldn't help worrying. I worried I'd crash into a car or trolley or someone else's bicycle, and I worried I'd get tired before anyone else. The only place I didn't worry was in Vondelpark.

Vondelpark is big and green with wide bike paths and no cars. It's full of couples, dogs, and old people. Not too many kids, though. And no colorful tulips because it's summertime. Holland must be extra beautiful in the spring—the postcard racks all show giant tulip fields filled with bright blooming flowers.

I loved loved loved not having to watch out for traffic. I also loved speeding up and making circles and doing wheelies and biking one-handed and going side by side with Cecily.

We got off our bikes to rest in a rose garden, and Matt made up a game that was like an outside version of No Peeking. He told Cecily to close her eyes, then he led her to a rose and told her to smell it and guess the color—red, yellow, pink, orange, or white. She kept guessing wrong and Matt kept cracking up.

I overheard Mom and Dad whispering about Cecily's mom's operation, which must be coming up pretty soon. Mom said, "I can't imagine what she's going through." I realized that I haven't been thinking at all about Mrs. Hausner. Maybe kids hardly ever think about grown-ups' problems? Or maybe some do? Or should?

Just then Mom called out, "Hey kids, who can spot a squirrel?"

That sounded easy, so Cecily, Matt, and I started looking. But we couldn't find any! Not one! In Central Park, we would have found bunches.

"Squirrels are rare in Europe," Mom said. She said that in New York, foreign tourists sometimes stop to take photos of squirrels.

Imagine thinking that a bushy-tailed squirrel is a big deal. Then again, Dutch people think biking in a busy city is not a big deal and it totally is!

We had dinner early. It was cheese fondu.

Cheese fondu is a bubbling hot pot of cheese melted with a lot of wine plunked in front of you right at your table. You put a piece of bread or apple at the end of a metal poker thing and stir it all around until it's covered with gloopy cheese. Then you blow on it and eat it.

Cecily loved it and Matt said he was glad the bread was soft since his tooth is so loose.

Mom said fondu means "melted" in French. "Do you like it, Melanie?" she asked.

"Not really," I said. "It's a little winy."

"Sometimes you're a little whiny and we like you," Dad said, smiling.

I could *not* believe Dad said that! Matt started laughing like a hyena. Even Cecily laughed a little.

I looked down at my empty plate and my eyes were stinging and I couldn't get the bread in my mouth to go past the lump in my throat and it was all I could do not to cry.

"Come on, cupcake," Dad said, putting his hand on my arm. "I'm just teasing."

"You're jet-lagged, pumpkin," Mom said. "Hang in there. We'll be going to bed soon."

"I'm not tired!" I said even though I probably was. After that I didn't say another word because I was afraid that if I looked up, the tears in my eyes would spill out. It also did not help that, right in front of Cecily, Dad had called me cupcake, Mom had called me pumpkin, and they both had been singing Beatles songs.

Mom got the check and said, "Well, *I'm* tired. Let's go."

I was hoping our luggage had arrived while we were out, but Hendrik, the check-in man, said nothing had been delivered.

I was about to complain, but Cecily said, "Oh well, at least it won't be hard to figure out what to wear tomorrow!"

Mom and Dad laughed and Dad said, "You're right about that!"

I bet they think Cecily has a great attitude.

Especially compared to you-know-who.

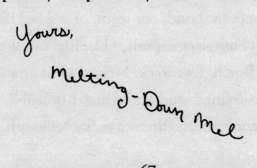

Yours,

Melting-Down Mel

P.S. Matt's asleep and Dad helped Cecily try to call her parents. She had to dial special numbers just to connect to America. Neither of her parents was home, though, so she left messages.

P.P.S. It turns out that Cecily packed her teddy, Snow Bear, right in her backpack. She's lucky. I'm about to go to bed holding a little balled-up washcloth. Talk about pitiful!

August 13
a cloudy morning
on a bus to Alkmaar (Ahlk Mar)

Dear Diary,

Even though I didn't have Hedgehog or my pajamas, and even though it was only early afternoon in New York, I fell right asleep last night. Our sofa bed is big and comfortable and neither of us snores, kicks, rolls, steals covers, grinds our teeth, or is a bed hog, so Cecily and I both slept slept slept like Rip Van Winkle.

He was Dutch. Last week, Mom read Matt and me Washington Irving's story about how Rip Van Winkle went up a mountain and drank a yucky brew with some

Dutchmen who were playing ninepins. But the men were actually the ghosts of Henry Hudson and his crew, and the drink was a magic potion that made him fall asleep. When he woke up, he was stiff and sore and he had a long white beard. He had slept for *twenty* years!

Well, we slept for *twelve* hours—from 8:00 P.M. to 8:00 A.M.

I think we might be almost on Holland time now, meaning that morning feels like morning (not the middle of the night) and evening feels like evening (not the middle of the day). I hope so—I'm tired of being tired!

The first thing I asked Mom this morning was "Has our lost luggage arrived?" She said, "No, darling."

It should have come by now! I want Hedgehog!!

Matt asked, "We're never never ever ever going to get our luggage, are we?"

Mom said we would.

I asked if we had to wear the same clothes AGAIN, and Mom said we had no choice, but if we wanted to take a shower and flip our underwear inside out, that might be a good idea.

I can't believe Mom said that. And in front of Cecily! It was *soooo* embarrassing, not to mention

Disgusto Deluxe!!!

"If our stuff doesn't arrive today, we should sue," I said. "Or at least buy new underwear."

Mom called the baggage people, but their number was busy. She asked the check-in man to call them while we are out.

I wrote two poems.

The first is:

Packing for a trip?
Here's a little tip:
Take a spare pair
Of underwear!

The second is the kind Miss Sands once made us do. Each line begins with a letter that helps spell a word— in this case, Holland.

H as
O ur
L ost
L uggage
A rrived?
N o,
D arling.

Well, we are now on our way to Alkmaar, a town known for its cheese market and cheese museum.

We are on a bus. Matt is sitting on Cecily's lap.

Cecily just said, "Matt, you have a bony butt," and Matt laughed like that was the greatest compliment you could ever hear. If I'd called Matt's butt bony, he would have hit me. Then I'd have hit him and we'd have gotten in a big fight and ended up in big trouble. But since it was Cecily calling his butt bony, Matt acted charmed.

I don't get it. And Matt doesn't even have a bony butt. He has a squooshy tushy. Or a plump rump.

The guide on our bus is young and cute. He has blond hair and grayish eyes. He gave me a brochure. He says "Hello" like "Hollow." He is explaining everything in Dutch, English, Spanish, and French. Mom said many Europeans speak several languages. She said that if people in Connecticut had their own language and people in New Jersey had their own language, maybe New Yorkers would learn Connecticutese and New Jerseyese, but since most Americans speak English, most don't try very hard to learn other languages.

"I speak pig latin," Cecily said. "Ig-pay atin-lay."

Mom smiled and said, "E-may oo-tay," which means "Me too." Mom told me that to speak pig latin, you take the first consonant of a word and move it to the end and add ay. So I said, "Ello-hay!" to Cecily, and she said, "Ello-hay, Elanie-may!" back to me.

Mom speaks Spanish, French, pretty good Italian, and okay pig latin. But even Mom says Dutch is difficult.

It sounds difficult.

For example, if you want to say "please," it's ~~absu~~ ~~aswu~~ alstublieft, which you pronounce Ahl Stoo Bleeft. (Sorry for the cross-outs. I had to ask Mom how to spell it because it is as impossible to spell as it is to say.)

It sounds sort of like "All stew is blecchh!" but last night when I was thirsty, I pointed to my empty water glass and said, "All stew is blecchh!" and the waitress looked at me as though I'd flown in from Pluto.

"Thank you" is easier. It's *dank u wel* (Don Coo Well).

"Yes" is *ja* (Ya) and "no" is *nee* (Nay).

Here's the point: I'm glad our guide speaks English! (I'm glad he's cute too!)

He asked me my name, and I said Melanie, and he said, "That's a pretty name," so I asked him his name, and he said Hans, and I said, "That's a handsome name." I couldn't believe I said that! I started to blush, and he just smiled (really cutely). Then Matt and Cecily introduced themselves and he ruffled Matt's hair and asked Cecily where she's from and said her name was pretty too!

Hans stood up at the front of the bus and told everyone to look out their windows. "You see that lovely green countryside? It used to be covered with water. We are driving along the bottom of an old dried-up lake." Then he said, "Cecily?"

She glanced at me and half giggling, answered, "Yes?"

"Cecily, what do you call my country?"

"Holland?" she answered.

"*Ja*, you call it Holland," he agreed. "But to us, North and South Holland are just two of twelve provinces. You see the bumper stickers on those cars? They say NL. We are the Netherlands. We are part of the Low Countries. Much of our land is low—below sea level!"

"*Below* the sea?" Matt asked.

"*Ja*, Matt," Hans said, and Matt sat up tall and proud. "Hundreds of years ago, we took the land back from the sea by building dikes and dams and using windmills to pump water out of the lakes. Who remembers my name?"

I raised my hand, but Cecily blurted out, "Hans."

"*Ja*. And who knows the book *Hans Brinker, or the Silver Skates?*"

"I do," Mom said. "It's written by an American woman."

"*Ja*. It's not Dutch at all," Hans smiled. "In the book, there's a story of a boy who sees water trickling through a hole in a dike—which is a low wall built to prevent floods. Come here, Matt." Matt stepped up and Hans got him to stick out his pointer finger. "That boy poked his finger in the hole to stop the leak," Hans continued, "and stayed that way all night and until the next morning, when a man saw him and helped him. He was a hero!" You could tell that Matt felt like a hero too, but then Hans told him to go sit down. "That story is make-believe. Today, we have modern ways to prevent floods."

I tried to picture myself saving the day and being a hero.

In front of me, Dad whispered, "I hope this excursion isn't a tourist trap."

Matt said, "What's an excursion?"

Dad said, "A field trip."

Matt said, "I love field trips. Especially the bus rides."

Cecily said, "What's a tourist trap?"

Dad said, "It's when tourists get lured to the same crowded place and the place isn't all that interesting."

"And they trap you?" Matt asked. His eyes got big and round and he stopped fiddling with his stupid baby tooth.

"No," Dad laughed. "They just take some of your money."

"If Alkmaar is a little touristy," Mom said, "that's fine because Matt here is a little tourist."

"I'm sure it'll be fun," Cecily said, all cheerful.

"I bet it will be cheesy," I piped in. I meant it as a joke. Cecily laughed but I could feel Mom and Dad just wishing I had a better attitude. Sometimes even I wish I had a better attitude.

I also wish Cecily would stop acting so cheerful. She's like a teacher's pet, only in this case, a family's pet. I thought it would be great being on vacation with her. But when we got on the bus and Matt said, "Sit next to me!" instead of saying, "Dream on, you little twerp," she looked right at me, then said, "Okay," and plopped next to him like she was *his* friend, not mine.

I can't believe Matt the Brat is taking over my best friend. I can't believe she's letting him. And I can't believe Hans called on Cecily and made Matt the star of his show when he knew me first.

Right now Cecily is letting Matt color all over her magazine. He is sitting on his bony-squooshy-plump butt-tushy-rump uglying up all the celebrities. He's giving them antlers and bloodshot eyes and drawing Band-Aids and Frankenstein stitches on their faces and putting cotton balls in some of their nostrils and making boogers ooze out of other of their nostrils. And Cecily is *laughing*.

Mom and Dad are sitting side by side reading a book of van Gogh's letters.

That leaves me, myself, and I in my slept-in clothes and inside-out underwear.

At least I've got you and a pencil. And Anne Frank's diary.

I'm up to the part where she says that she knows it does no good to be "gloomy" but says, "Still, I can't refrain from telling you that lately I have begun to feel deserted. . . . But why do I bother you with such foolish things? I'm very ungrateful, Kitty; I know that."

I feel a little deserted too. But, I know that I should be very grateful.

It's just hard sometimes.

Bye,
Elanie-may

on the bus to ~~Rotterdam~~ Zaanse Schans
(Zon Za HHHunse)

Dear Diary,

I guess I'm just not as into cheese as some people.

I mean, cheese is okay. I like American cheese, and cream cheese on bagels, and mozzarella on pizza, and sometimes I don't mind a sprinkle of parmesan on spaghetti.

But I'm not a cheese person.

Well, around here, they take cheese very seriously—too seriously.

Hans took us to a cheese museum—a *kaasmuseum* (Cahs Moo Zay Um). Cecily walked on one side of Hans and I walked on the other.

We went to a cheese market that's been going on every Friday morning pretty much forever. Cheese sellers in straw hats were auctioning off tons of huge yellow cheeses. Imagine if you put your arms out in a big circle and touched your fingertips. Each wheel of cheese is that big—maybe bigger. Hans looked at me and asked, "You know what these cheeses are covered with?"

I wanted to say *"Ja,"* but shook my head. I wished

78

he'd given me an easy question.

"Wax," Hans said. We watched the men stack the waxy cheeses onto wooden sleds and rush to get them weighed and sent all over the world. Probably even to New York.

"Holland was the first country to export cheese," Hans said. "Holland still exports more cheese than any other country."

"Sports?" Matt said. "What's x-sports?"

"Exports," Dad explained, "are things one country sells to another country."

Cecily asked Hans to take a picture of all five of us in front of the giant cheeses. He gave her a big smile, and to make sure we smiled, guess what he told us to say?

— — — — — — ○

Speaking of, Mom and Dad bought a plate of cheese for us to sample. I didn't want any. Matt said, "Pretend you're a mouse. *Now* do you want some?"

I glared at him and said, "Pretend you're a human. *Now* will you mind your own beeswax?"

Matt swung his arm out, to punch me, I think, and he banged his elbow on a gate and ripped his shirt.

79

(Served him right.) He started hopping around and moaning, "Ow ow ow ow ow!" and Cecily hugged him and said, "Matt, you poor thing. There's nothing funny about funny bones, is there?"

I swear, I felt like puking.

At lunch, I practically did puke. We had pumpernickel bread with pea soup, or *erwtensoep*, which Mom pronounces Air Tin Soup.

I thought it was gross. Cecily loved it. (Naturally.)

Matt told Cecily his favorite joke. He told her to say "pea green soup" after everything he said.

Matt said, "What did you have for breakfast?"

Cecily said, "Pea green soup."

"What did you have for lunch?"

"Pea green soup."

"What are you having for dinner?"

"Pea green soup."

"What are you going to do before you go to bed?"

"Pea green soup!"

Everybody laughed.

Except me.

1. That joke is immature.

80

2. I've heard it about a billion times.

3. I don't like pea soup for breakfast, lunch, or dinner.

Gaggingly yours,
Lem

P.S. I signed my name backwards because everything feels sort of wrong right now.

early afternoon on the bus back to

Dear Diary,   *Amster Amster DaM DaM DaM*

I feel as if I'm getting smaller and smaller. Like Alice in Wonderland or something.

Hans isn't paying attention to any of us. He's talking different languages to a bunch of adults. He's probably telling *all* the ladies that they have pretty names.

He led us to a cheese shop where a blond lady in a puffy white costume talked in Dutch and English about how cheese is made. Matt whispered, "It stinks in here." Mom said, "Shhhh," and the lady explained that cheesemakers boil milk, then add "lactic acid" and

81

"rennet" so the milk curdles and separates into curds and whey.

"Curds and whey?" Matt said. "That's what Little Miss Muffet eats!"

Dad laughed and Mom beamed at her little Angel Boy, and the lady kept talking about smelly cheeses. She said cheese can be eaten "young" or ripened in salt water and eaten months or years later. She said aging cheese makes it more flavorful.

Petrified cheese? Flavorful?

Yuck!

All this curds-and-whey talk wasn't making me hungry; it was making me want to hold my nose.

Dad must have seen me squinch up my face because he announced, "Melanie likes her cheese bright orange, square, processed, individually wrapped, and made in the good ol' U. S. of A."

First of all, since when is that a crime? Second, since when does everyone else care about young versus old cheese, and sheep versus goat cheese?

I thought Cecily might defend me because she likes golden brown grilled American cheese sandwiches as much as I do. But she giggled along with Dad. She was giving Matt a piggyback ride and they were sampling bites of Gouda. The Dutch lady pronounced it Howda, or HHHGHHHowda, as if she were gargling and the word got stuck in her throat and she finally had to spit it out.

When the lady walked away, Dad said, "Howdy, kids! Howda like the Howda?" Matt made a thumbs-up sign and he and Cecily started saying "HHHGH-HHowda HHHGHHHowda HHHGHHHowda."

Then Matt whispered, "Who cut the cheese?"

Cecily said, "He who smelt it dealt it."

Matt said, "She who denied it supplied it."

I wasn't going to laugh, but I looked at Dad and couldn't help smiling.

Cecily laughed this morning when Dad said he was going to "shake a tower" (meaning take a shower). He's been using that line since I was *born*, so none of us *ever* laughs when he says it. But Cecily had never heard it. You could tell it just made Dad's day to have someone appreciate his ancient comedy routine.

Cecily might have figured out that I'm mad at her because she asked me if I was. We were standing near some old wooden windmills. One used wind power to grind stuff into mustard and the other used wind power to grind stuff into paint. (Holland has about a thousand windmills.) Well, we all went up and down the musty mustard mill. Then Matt and Mom and Dad went up the paint windmill but Cecily and I didn't because we saw two Dutch children feeding two little goats.

We walked over and Cecily said, "Aren't they cute?"
I just shrugged. I felt like saying,

If you'd like to have a chat,
Go and talk to Matt the BRAT.

But I knew that would be immature, so I didn't.

Even though I did a good job of not being immature, I did not do a good job of being mature because I didn't say anything at all.

That's when Cecily asked, "Are you mad at me?"

I was so surprised, I said, "No."

After that I didn't know what to say, which is weird since at home we talk nonstop when we're together, and when we're on the phone, neither of us wants to be the first to hang up so we sometimes say "Bye! Bye! Bye! Bye! Bye! Bye!" until one of our moms forces us to put down the phone.

Well, we just stood there in silence, because I couldn't exactly accuse her of stealing my family or Hans away. After a while, Cecily said *"Hallo"* to the Dutch children and they said *"Hallo"* back. Then

Mom, Dad, and Matt showed up and Dad said, "Two American kids, two Dutch kids, and two goat kids—this calls for a photo!"

Mom said, "Smile and say you-know-what."

Cecily and I did smile and say you-know-what. But I didn't feel like it and I bet she didn't either.

All Smiled Out,

M. :(

P.S. *I did not think that we would fight.*

I thought that things would turn out right.

afternoon at the canal house

Dear Diary,

I just took my first ever horse-and-buggy ride!! (In New York, Mom and Dad always say that it's too expensive.)

Our buggy had red flowers in the front and big back wheels with long spokes and skinny tires and our horse was black and had blinders and a nice barn smell. His name was Bert. Not like Bert and Ernie, though. More like Bearrrrt. Well, guess what? *He understood Dutch!* The driver, whose name was Wouter (Vow Ter), spoke Dutch to him and English to us! He told Cecily and me to sit right up front next to him, and he even let us take turns holding the reins! The horse went clip-clopping past churches, down quiet alleyways, on busy streets, and next to canals.

Going around Amsterdam by bicycle is fun, but going by horse is even funner.

More fun.

Whatever.

It was also fun to be sitting *next* to Cecily for a change.

At first, sitting next to her without talking made it extra obvious that we were both feeling uncomfortable (and I don't mean because of the lumpy cushions). But then the driver stopped the buggy at a vegetable stand to buy three carrots for us kids to give to his horse later. He said, "You take care of Bert, *ja?*" so I nodded.

Suddenly, two teenage guys with spiky purple hair and shoulder tattoos and eyebrow rings crossed the street in front of us. I thought up a comment, and wasn't sure if I should say it, but then I blurted out, "I think I'm in luuuvvv!"

"*Ja*, me too!" Cecily said. "I hof a feeling in my heart that I hof never felt before!"

I pretended to look worried. "But what of Christopher's heart? Will it not break in two when he finds out?"

Cecily eyed the spiky-haired teenagers and said, "Christopher? Who is this Christopher?"

We started laughing and soon I had to wipe my eyes as if I'd been crying. It's not that what we were saying was so funny. It's just that it was soooo nice to be joking around again.

A pregnant lady walked by and Cecily said, "Remember when I put the basketball under my shirt in gym and pretended to be having a baby?"

"*Ja*," I said. "Remember when I put two green tennis balls up my shirt and pretended to be Miss America?"

"*Ja*," she said. "Remember that piñata at your birthday party and how we had to whack it a billion times?

And when it finally cracked open, all the hard candies had broken into tiny bits and all the gooey candies had slimed over everything?"

"*Ja*," I said. "Remember when we buried an ant alive but then we felt bad so we tried to unbury it?"

The more we remembered, the more we laughed. The buggy driver came back and he looked at us and said, "Fun, *ja*?" so we smiled and said, "*Ja*" again. But the truth is, I'd almost forgotten about him and his horse! It was as if Cecily and I were in our own world. Just us.

After a while, the driver pulled the buggy to the side of the road and we all got out and Mom took a picture of us feeding Bert his carrot snacks (unpeeled, of course). Then Matt pulled a bag of M&M's out of his pocket and said, "Cecily, I have a snack for you," and spilled a few into her palm.

"Thanks, Matt," she said. "Hey, look! All blues—my favorite!"

"Really?" Matt said. "Mine too!" He gave her a huuuuge hug, and she threw her M&M's in the air and caught them one by one in her mouth, and he cheered every time.

Well, I hate to even write this, but for some reason, I suddenly felt like the buggy ride had been a beautiful soap bubble . . . and it had just popped.

Your friend,
mel

bedtime

Dear Diary,

Dinner was ~~res~~ rijsttafel, which means rice table, which Mom pronounces Rays Tahffle.

It all started in Indonesia. Dad said that long ago when Amsterdam was the most important port in the whole entire world, the Dutch East Indies Company was always sailing back and forth to the Far East, and next thing you know, people in Holland had Indonesian spices and ingredients to cook with, and they started making up new recipes.

Here's how ~~ris~~ rijsttafel works: The waiter puts a long, skinny, hot plate on your table, then brings tons of little dishes of food. Everything from fried coconuts, fried bananas, sweet potatoes, cut-up cucumbers, and nuts to chicken kebabs, pork in soy sauce, beef on a stick, and shrimp bread. Fortunately he also brings a big bowl of rice (otherwise, I personally might have starved to death).

Well, ~~admittedly~~ rijsttafel may be a big-deal specialty, but I didn't like it.

Cecily loved it. So Mom and Dad went on and on (again!) about how great she is at trying things. I can't believe I never knew she was an "adventurous eater"— as Dad keeps putting it. Meanwhile, he keeps telling me not to be a "grumble bee."

I also can't believe I get jealous whenever Mom and Dad compliment her and criticize me. Maybe I truly am a bad person. Or maybe they're being unfair.

In Anne Frank's diary, she wrote that her parents "never rebuke" her sister, Margot, and "always" scold her about everything. That's what it's like for me! Precious Matt never gets in trouble, and, of course, Cecily can do no wrong.

Well, before Mom or Dad could stop him, Matt did something wrong. He tried an Indonesian sauce he thought was ketchup. It wasn't. It was hot peppery *sambal* (Some Bull). Matt turned red and had to wash the sauce down with about fifty glasses of water. I was about to laugh, but I was afraid we were all going to have to rush to another emergency room.

Matt kept drinking water until he felt halfway normal again. (I doubt Matt ever feels totally normal.)

And I wrote a haiku.

> What if we had an
> Amsterdam emergency?
> Would 911 work?

On the way home from the restaurant, we stopped to see the streetlights and bridge lights and boat lights reflected in the dark canal. It was soooo pretty. Cecily said, "Look, the moon is glistening in the water!" Mom just loved that.

I spotted the first star in the night sky, so I silently made a wish. I wished I would stop being mad at Cecily.

Meanwhile, Matt, Mr. Fifty Glasses of Water, said, "I have to pee!" so we all started walking again.

Suddenly, out of nowhere, about a zillion rollerbladers

whizzed by. We stepped back and watched. They were mostly young men, but some were old men, some were women, and some were kids. Not too many were wearing helmets, but some were wearing blades that gave off sparks, like miniature fireworks. It was very cool.

Matt was wriggling and saying, "Let's go," but we couldn't cross the street until they finished blurring by. Mom asked a lady what was going on and she said Friday-night rollerblading is a tradition.

I said, "It's amazing: Dutch people used to clop around in wooden shoes and now they race around on wheels!"

I thought that was an interesting comment, and Dad would have too—if Cecily had said it. But since *I* said it, he said, "True. But then, the Dutch have always been expert skaters, and rollerblading is like ice-skating on pavement."

Well, it's pure good luck that we got to see them on our second evening in Holland.

But it's pure bad luck that . . . our luggage still hasn't come!

When we got back, the check-in man said it may take another day or two.

Dad blew up!

"Another day or two! That's outrageous!" he said. "We're here for only a week!"

Hendrik said nobody was at the baggage office at this hour, but if we don't get our luggage by tomorrow, the company will have to compensate us for our inconvenience.

"What does that mean?" Matt asked.

"Give us some money for new clothes," Mom said.

"Does luggage ever stay lost?" I asked.

"Rarely," Mom said.

Matt looked at me and I explained that "rarely" is grown-up for "sometimes."

Matt is worried about DogDog, and I'm worried about Hedgehog!

As we walked up the steep stairway of the canal house, Mom and Dad got grouchier with every step. They said that if our stuff doesn't come while we're asleep, we'll go shopping first thing tomorrow.

I won't mind shopping.

I like shopping.

Dad doesn't. He said he didn't come to Amsterdam to

go shopping and he doesn't want to spend all day at it.

Mom said, "Sweetheart, I didn't come for the shopping either. I came for the art, and if nobody objects, I wouldn't mind seeing some paintings, *dank u wel*." She wants to see the Van Gogh Museum, Rembrandt's house, the Rijksmuseum (Rakes Moo Zay Um), and the modern art museum, for starters.

Dad said, "Honey, be realistic. We can't possibly do everything, especially with three kids."

Mom said, "I won't have my children growing up thinking that Dutch Masters is just the name of a cigar company."

Dad said, "Miranda, they already know better—and this is supposed to be a vacation, for God's sake." (He said for God's sake, not for gosh sake.)

It was embarrassing that Mom and Dad were arguing in front of Cecily. Usually they behave better when other people are around. I whispered to Cecily that my parents always call each other sweetheart and honey when they argue, and Cecily smiled a tiny bit.

Matt started crying—I don't know whether it was because of Dad and Mom arguing or because of DogDog being lost or because of burning the roof of his mouth or because he was about to pee in his pants and it was taking Dad forever to unlock the door.

Cecily, for once, *didn't* tell everyone not to worry. The funny thing is, I kind of wish she had.

Cecily is my best friend.
I do not want that to end.
I liked sitting side by side,
Laughing on the buggy ride.

Dad finally got the door open and Matt ran to the bathroom and Cecily kicked off her sandals and said, "I'm going to shake a tower." Dad, of course, laughed— ho ho ho like jolly old Saint Nick.

Then Matt started moaning about DogDog, and *Cecily lent him Snow Bear for the night.* Matt and Dad and Mom were all touched. I was nauseated.

Maybe I should never have invited Cecily on this trip.

But then, *I* didn't.

Mom did.

Maybe Mom thought that having Cecily here would

help us all get along. Wrong! (Or partly wrong anyway. Everyone else *is* mostly getting along.)

Or maybe Mom really just wanted to help Cecily's mom. I keep forgetting that Cecily's mom is very sick. I bet Cecily hasn't forgotten, though.

Good Night —
Smelly Mellie

P.S. I wrote Smelly Mellie because I can't believe I'm still wearing these clothes. As for Dad . . .

Dad is still in his same old clothes.
When he walks by, just hold your nose.

P.P.S. Cecily tried to call home but her mom wasn't there, so she left another message. Right now Cecily is being sort of quiet. I wonder if she wishes she hadn't lent Snow Bear to Matt the Brat.

August 14

late morning at the canal house

Dear Diary,

What woke me up today was Dad making phone calls about our luggage. He found out that our luggage was definitely on the plane with us. The luggage people's computers were down but now they are working again, so they said they would be able to trace our stuff.

"Then do it!" Dad said, sounding sort of mean. "We're losing patience."

Cecily raised her eyebrows at me. Normally I might have raised my eyebrows back, but I didn't feel like agreeing with her that my dad was mean. It's one thing for me to notice, but another for her to.

When I didn't make a matching face, Cecily turned her head away.

Dad slammed down the phone and said, "What a bunch of nitwits."

At least he didn't start cursing.

"What's a nitwit?" Matt asked.

Dad should probably have been a teacher, like

98

Mom, because as soon as he began explaining, he got in a better mood. "Nitwit means dumdum," Dad said. "The word may come from when the children of Dutch settlers had to go to school even though they couldn't speak English. When teachers called on them, the poor kids kept saying "*Niet weten*'" (Neat Vay Ten), which is Dutch for 'I don't know.' Pretty soon, other kids started making fun of them and calling them nitwits."

"That's not very nice," Matt said.

"Children sometimes aren't," Mom said as she walked into our room. I couldn't tell if she meant any of us. "Ready to go shopping?" she asked.

"Well, we're dressed!" Cecily said. Everyone laughed because we're always dressed. We go to sleep dressed and we wake up dressed.

Mom said, "Cecily, I'm impressed that your shirt still looks so clean. Can you imagine if Matt had worn white?"

Matt looked down and smiled as though three days of food stains and a big elbow hole are something to be proud of.

We went down to the canal house kitchen for breakfast. There were different kinds of cereal and I started remembering how Mrs. Hausner used to help Cecily and me make Froot Loops necklaces with licorice strings. It was a nice memory, but it made me feel sad. Now Mrs. Hausner is sick (and probably disappointed in me) and Cecily and I act like we're hardly even friends.

I poured myself a bowl of Rice Krispies. The box had Snap, Crackle, and Pop, and some Dutch words on it. Mom studied them as if she were doing a puzzle, then guessed that *"Een goed begin van de dag"* (Ayn Hooot Buh Hin Fun Duh Dahhgghh) might mean "A good beginning of the day."

Today did *begin* okay. We got on our rental bicycles and peddled past the Floating Flower Market, which Mom said is usually bright with flowers. Since it's August, though, there were mostly just flower bulbs. Trillions of little brown bulbs that looked like baby onions but with pictures of flowers next to them. I thought it was amazing how something as pretty as a flower could come from something as plain as a bulb. Mom bought a few and said, "Some bulbs make flowers that bloom and die and bloom again."

Maybe my friendship with Cecily is like that. Maybe it's not really over.

Knowing Mom, she probably *said* the thing about bulbs so I would *think* the thing about friendship. Teachers can do stuff like that!

We bicycled to a department store on a street that doesn't allow cars, and we locked up our bicycles. Mom said we could each buy underwear, pajamas, a bathing suit, and a new outfit—courtesy of the luggage people.

Well, we started trying on clothes a mile a minute so Dad wouldn't get impatient. Cecily and I did *not* share a dressing room, but we did model all the clothes for each other. She looked great in almost everything and I looked not great in almost everything.

We are now all back in the canal house changing. I can't believe how happy I was just to change.

Mom too. She threw out Matt's old shirt and said she'd been afraid we'd be wearing the same clothes in every one of our vacation photos.

Even though I'm glad to be wearing a new top and new shorts, I'm mad because no one said anything about them. Mom complimented Cecily on her new clothes and went on and on about how pretty she looks in blue. Mom even said, "Royal blue is a wonderful color on you, Cecily."

Every color is a wonderful color on Cecily.

Every color is a royal color on Princess Cecily.

Doesn't anyone think red is a wonderful color on Mediocre Melanie?

If I don't say something soon to Mom or Cecily, I might explode.

Anne Frank wrote, "I'm boiling with rage, and yet I mustn't show it."

I can relate.

Dag. (That means bye.)

Melanie the invisible

Dear Diary,

All aboard! Cecily and Matt are playing Uno, Dad is reading, and I am writing. Mom isn't with us because we split up for the afternoon. She's going to the history museum and modern art museum with a Culture Pass she bought that gets her in everywhere. Since today is beauuuutiful, Dad is taking us to visit a nearby city, Haarlem, and a nearby beach.

Dad said that New York's Harlem was named for Holland's Haarlem and was started by a peg-legged Dutch guy named Peter Stuyvesant. But Holland's Haarlem has two a's and New York's has only one. Mom added that New York's Harlem was a center of jazz and art and the home of the poet Langston Hughes. She and Dad always like to tack on extra facts.

Uh-oh, I can't believe we're *already* pulling into the Haarlem station!!

BYE 4 NOW
MEL

103

on a pew in St. Bavokerk in Haarlem

Dear Diary,

Matt was walking really slowly and Dad kept saying "Hurry!" and Matt kept saying "Wait up!" Finally Cecily said, "Hey Matt, what do you get when you cross a turtle and a porcupine?" Matt shrugged his shoulders. "What?" Cecily said, "A slow poke!" and we all laughed. Even me.

I hope things are getting back to normal again. When things feel wrong, it makes me worry that Dad might have a point: Maybe I don't appreciate it enough when things feel right.

I wonder if Anne Frank appreciated her life when she was ten and a half. In her diary, she tries so hard to have a good attitude. She says their hiding place is "a paradise compared with how other Jews who are not in hiding must be living."

And she really appreciates the friends who help them and bring them stuff. She wrote, "Miep is just like a pack mule, she fetches and carries so much. . . . We always long for Saturdays when our books come. Just like little children receiving a present. Ordinary people simply don't know what books mean to us, shut up here."

It makes me wonder: Was Anne Frank ever just an ordinary person? Did she ever visit Haarlem or have a fight with her best friend?

I'll tell you this. We *are* appreciating Haarlem because it is soooo pretty! Dad took a ton of pictures of the brick alleyways and antique-y street lamps and the flowers in the courtyard of the Frans Hals Museum. Cecily liked the museum. I didn't because it was mostly full of portraits of old fogies who have been dead forever.

We did see one painting we all liked so much that we bought Mom a postcard of it. Jan Breughel (Yahn Brew Gull) painted it around 1640 and it's called *Allegory of Tulipomania*. Tulipomania sounds like a disease but isn't. It was when people got so excited about tulips that came in new shapes or colors that they spent gazillions of guilders (old Dutch money) to buy bulbs. Someone once paid as much for one bulb as it would have cost to buy an entire house!! But rich people liked having fancy tulips in their gardens because then everyone could see how rich they were. Meanwhile regular people thought they were out of their minds, and ministers gave sermons about how it's wrong to spend so much on flowers.

Well, in the painting (and postcard), dozens of *monkeys*, not human beings, are buying and selling tulips and bulbs. One monkey is peeing on tulips! (That cracked Matt up.) Dad said that was Breughel's way of making fun of rich people. He also said that Breughel's father and uncle were really famous painters. (I'd never heard of them.)

We are now in a church that is around five hundred years old. I'm sitting down because my feet feel five hundred years old.

Mozart played the organ here when he was ten. Can you believe he was famous when he was my age? (I *have* heard of Mozart!)

I am now going to shut my eyes and try to imagine what his organ concert sounded like. I am also going to try to picture him wearing one of those white wigs with a ponytail attached.

If my signature is funny, it's because my eyes will be closed.

Do Re Mi—

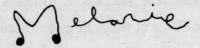

on the train to Zandvoort (Sand Fort)

Dear Diary,

I got in trouble.

We three kids wanted fast food, but Dad said no, so we went to this tiny fancy place and ordered pork chops and *stamppot* (Stamp Pot is mashed potatoes and mixed-up vegetables). Dad also ordered a beer by saying, "I'll have a Heinie" (for Heineken). I felt like hiding under the table!

My pork chop was good except it had gristle and fat on it, so after I ate everything I liked, I pushed the disgusting stuff to one side of my plate. But even there, it was still grossing me out, so I spooned up the gristle and fat and dumped it onto Dad's plate.

Okay, fine, I realize I don't have the World's Best Manners. But first of all, they're not as bad as Matt's. And second of all, I *always* separate yummy stuff from yucky stuff and transfer the yucky stuff to Dad's plate, and he *never* minds. A lot of times he even thanks me! At home, when we order in fried rice, I transfer heaping spoonfuls of egg and onions to Dad's plate, and he gobbles up my rejects, happy as can be. (He is a Big Pig, after all.)

The problem was that this time when I transferred the food, I accidentally splashed sauce onto Dad's new striped shirt.

Next thing you know, his striped shirt was polka-dotted with brownish-orangeish specks. Dad quietly checked the damage and took a deep breath. I expected him to start ranting about how after wearing the same dirty shirt for days, he finally gets to put on something clean and new and I go and make a mess of it. Or how my table manners are atrocious and I should be ashamed and wait till Mom hears about this. Or *something*.

Maybe it was because the restaurant was tiny, but Dad stayed quiet. I looked at Cecily and Matt to see if they were smiling or making faces, but they were both staring straight down.

I almost wanted Dad to just start yelling because, well, imagine knowing a volcano is going to explode but not knowing *when*.

Finally, it occurred to me to say, "Sorry, Dad."

Using his inside voice, Dad said, "Thank you for apologizing, Melanie. But I do not want you to use my plate as a garbage can anymore. Is that clear?" He was rubbing bubbly water on his shirt.

I nodded, but Dad repeated, "Is that clear?" so I said, "Yes." I even said "Sorry" again because I was.

My eyes were burning and I was hoping I wouldn't start crying with Cecily right there. But then I did start and I had to keep dabbing my eyes with my napkin and hoping no one noticed even though everyone probably did.

Pathetically yours,

No-manners Mel

a little later

Dear Diary,

Anne Frank wrote in her diary, "Am I really so bad-mannered, conceited, headstrong, pushing, stupid, lazy, etc., etc., as they all say? Oh, of course not. I have my faults, just like everyone else, but they thoroughly exaggerate everything."

I want to keep reading, but our train is slowing down.

Time to get off! Holland is so small that we're already here at the North Sea. Sea in Dutch is *zee*.

Zeeeyou —
Mel

Dear Diary,

under a beach umbrella

Oh my God, I mean gosh! Mom may be seeing Rembrandts and Mondrians and de Koonings or whoever, but guess what we're seeing? Half-naked people!!! A lot of ladies on this beach are *not* wearing tops!!! They're wearing bikini bottoms and nothing else!!!

It's pretty embarrassing!!!

I wonder if Mom would even approve of Dad's taking us here—especially without her. Well, too late.

Here we are.

Dad is *not* concentrating on his guidebook. And when we got changed into our new bathing suits, he forgot to say one word about sunscreen. Usually he and Mom are *obsessed* with sunscreen. Usually they put sunscreen on the part on the top of my scalp, for ~~God's~~ gosh sake!

I have to admit that the beach ladies *are* pretty distracting! You can see their you-know-whats, which, if you ask me, is *completely* inappropriate. And some of the ladies are, well, *ancient* and saggy-baggy.

Matt keeps whispering to Cecily and laughing

111

uncontrollably. But she isn't laughing along. In fact, she walked over to me and away from Matt.

Matt just asked Dad, "Why are the ladies showing off their boobies?" Instead of getting mad, Dad answered that customs and culture are different here and that many Europeans are more open and comfortable with their bodies than many Americans.

Comfortable?! All I can say is, their comfortableness makes me *un*comfortable—and I don't mean because I have sand where I wish I didn't.

I broke the silence between me and Cecily. I said, "Cecily, how would you rate this beach? PG-13 or R?"

"I think PG-13," she said. "It's like *National Geographic*."

"*Ja*. I think you're right," I said, and we halfway smiled at each other.

In shock,

Melanie, WHO Is Wearing a TOP

Dear Diary,

The Holland beach was very hot,
So lots of ladies plain forgot
That in public it is best
To be fully— not halfway—dressed.

poetically yours,
Melanie

bedtime

Dear Diary,

At the canal house, Mom saw Dad's shirt and said, "What happened?" Dad looked right at me and said, "We had a little lunchtime incident. We've talked about it." Fortunately, Mom didn't ask any more questions (not in front of me anyway). We gave her the monkey-tulip-peepee postcard and told her about the half-nudie beach and she looked at Dad

113

and sort of laughed. That was good. I thought she might get mad.

Dinner was mussels and a mushy vegetable stew called *hutspot*. It is pronounced like Put Spot but with an H. Good thing there was also bread on the table!

Anyway, Cecily is talking to the rest of my family and they're talking to her, and she and I are talking a little, but things are still messed up between us. It's as if we haven't been properly introduced.

Sometimes I feel mad at Cecily and I think it's her fault. Other times I feel like I'm letting her down even though I don't really know how.

Right now Cecily is in the shower. Mom just came in with a coffee-table book of still lifes—paintings of gorgeous flowers surrounded by bugs buzzing and butterflies flying. She asked Matt to pick any page.

He picked a page, but the book was dusty, so he sneezed and then said, "Bless me!"

Mom smiled and asked, "What do you think the artist was trying to say?"

"How should I know?" Matt said. I stayed silent.

Mom went straight into Art-Teacher Mode. "Tomorrow these flowers won't be quite as beautiful, and soon their petals will fall. Even the insects will die. See?" I sort of saw. "I think the artist is saying," Mom continued, "'Appreciate being alive. Life is beautiful and delicate and fragile and it does not last forever.'"

Then Mom shut the book and tucked us in and said she'd be back in a minute to say good night to Cecily too.

Well, I don't know about Matt, but her little spiel kind of creeped me out. Who wants to think about life and death stuff when you're on vacation?

I hope I don't have bad dreams.

All Zee best,
Mel

August 15

early morning at the canal house

Dear Diary,

I didn't have bad dreams but I didn't sleep that well because Cecily kept mumbling and tossing and turning and accidentally kicking me. Once, her entire arm splatted across my face. I had to pick it up and drop it back onto her side of the bed. When I woke up, I was scrunched waaaay over on one side of the bed. It was a miracle I hadn't fallen off.

Tiredly (Is that a word?),

M.

a little later

Dear Diary,

The more I read Anne Frank's diary, the worse I feel about complaining about Cecily, Matt, Mom, and Dad. I mean, Anne was stuck with her family (two parents and one sister), *plus* another family (two parents and their teenage son), *plus* an old man dentist who shared a room with her! And they definitely weren't on vacation—they were in hiding!

Even though I wrote "I can relate," I think I've been clueless about her life and how depressing and scary it was. Anne wrote that sometimes she thinks of other

Jewish children who were taken away and feels "wicked sleeping in a warm bed." Well, I feel wicked for being a kid on vacation who forgets how good she has it and whines about stupid stuff.

Anne also wrote, "Would anyone, either Jew or non-Jew, understand this about me, that I am simply a young girl badly in need of some rollicking fun?"

I would! I feel so bad for her!

She would have loved to be in my shoes.

Frankly yours,
Melanie Martin, Diary Writer

12 noon
at a restaurant

Dear Diary,

Mom told Dad that she was going to Rembrandt's house, and that Dad should rent a canal bike with us, stay away from topless beaches (!), and meet her in two hours at the Rijksmuseum. (She knew 2 museums in 1 day would be 2 much 4 us.)

"Kids, be good," Mom said.

We said we'd try, but I think being good might not be my specialty.

A canal *bike* is a *boat* that you pedal with your feet.

I thought pedaling down the canals would be as fun as clip-clopping down the streets. But our bike-boat was a four-seater, and Matt immediately said, "Cecily, sit with me." Cecily looked right right right at me. It was like she expected me to say something, but I didn't know what. I almost said "No, sit with me!" but I didn't want her or Dad to say "Matt asked first." Well, she sat with Brat Boy, so guess who got stuck in the second row with Dad (no offense to Dad or anything)?

This is *not* how I pictured our trip!

Matt started pretending he was a tour guide (ha! a shrimpy one with freckles and a loose tooth!). He was talking with a Dutch accent and making stuff up about every bridge. Under one, he said, "Zees is a luffly example uf Dutch archeeetecshure." Cecily encouraged him by laughing her head off.

I didn't laugh once. To be honest, I ignored Cecily

and I called Matt a nitwit. I even whispered that the canals were full of starving pointy-toothed alligators that, if Matt fell in, would take bites out of his heart and eat his guts right up.

Matt looked scared, and said, "You're mean," and for half a second I worried that I was. But then Cecily mumbled something to Matt, and he said, "Alligators like *hot* places, not *cold* places," and he smiled at Cecily and stuck his tongue out at me. Then he made his hands into snapping alligator jaws and started pinching me, saying, "My fingers are pinching machines."

I don't know how much longer I can stand this! Matt is a dumdum and Cecily is part bunny, part tiger, and I had an urge to push them both overboard into the alligator-infested (not) water.

Well, I wanted to go to Pizza Hut, but Dad said no, so we went to a fish restaurant and I had spaghetti and it was okay, but my tomato sauce had too many lumps in it.

Lumpily,
meanie

P.S. That's my name without the L and that might be my personality too.

P.P.S. Did I tell you that our luggage didn't come this morning either? This is day four!! Even Mom and Dad seemed surprised.

P.P.P.S. Matt saw my P.S. and P.P.S. and started making peepee jokes.

6:00 P.M. at the canal house

Dear Diary,

Cecily and I just had the

BIGGEST FIGHT!

We had it in the Rijksmuseum, which is like the Metropolitan Museum back home. It is a "must-see" that is huge and quiet and full of tourists and old paintings.

It is *not* a very ideal place to have a fight, but it's not like I started it on purpose.

Here's what happened.

We met Mom in the entrance or *ingang* (In Hahng),

which is spelled like "Come in, gang!" Then we headed upstairs to the Rembrandt section. Mom was talking about how Rembrandt was the greatest painter who ever lived and how he kept getting better and better and how she was glad she saw his house and sketches and how he painted piles of portraits of himself, from when he was young to when he was old. Mom said that some of his self-portraits are so honest, you almost feel impolite when you look away. She said he left a whole "autobiography in paint."

I said, "I wonder if an artist who paints self-portraits is like a writer who keeps diaries."

I thought Mom would like that question, but she just said, "They didn't have cameras back then, so painting was a way to record what people and things looked like."

She showed Cecily and me this "masterpiece" of Rembrandt's mother reading the Bible. The mother's face is all ghosty, so I said, "It's not all that good."

Cecily disagreed. She said to look at the tiny wrinkles on her hand and the gold threads on her bonnet. She said she thought the painting was "haunting."

Haunting? *Pleeeease!*

Next Mom showed us this other masterpiece of these guys who ran a clothing business. I said, "What's so great about six funny-looking men with funny-looking white collars and funny-looking black hats?"

Cecily said to look at them looking at us. "It is hard to turn away from them, isn't it, Miranda? They seem so real, I half expect them to start talking to us."

I almost said, "If they *start* talking, maybe they'll tell you to *stop* talking." (I didn't say it, though. I just thought it really loudly.)

Finally, Mom took us to see the most famous masterpiece of all, this giant painting called *The Night Watch*. Mom said a bunch of soldiers hired Rembrandt to paint them, but instead of doing a group portrait with everyone all the same size, he painted an action painting with some soldiers big and up front, and others small and in the background. "Unfortunately," Mom said, "the soldiers did not like it at all."

"Me neither," I said. "And it's too big."

Mom looked so exasperated that I almost felt bad

for her. It was like she couldn't figure out where she'd gone wrong raising me.

Cecily loved the painting. "Check out the man's hand!" she said. "The light on his palm and his fingers makes his hand stick out like it's 3-D. It's like *he* wants to shake *our* hands!"

"Exactly," Mom said. It was a miracle she didn't add, "Melanie, why can't you appreciate Rembrandt like Cecily? And doesn't she look *lovely* in royal blue?"

Well, I looked around and I *did* appreciate some of the other paintings, like *The Holy Family at Night* and *The Jewish Bride*. I was even about to say so, but just then Matt came running over. He said that he and Dad saw a cool painting of children teaching a cat to dance ("Jan Steen," Dad said) and another of bundled-up skaters ("Avercamp," Dad said), but his favorite was of this guy's chopped-off bloody head served up on a tray. (Gross!)

"This guy," Dad explained, "was John the Baptist." Mom smiled. She loves when Matt and I pay attention to art—even if it's only because a scene is bloody or a statue is naked.

She led us to a small room that had paintings by Jan Vermeer in it. While Mom dug out paper and colored pencils from her backpack, she told us that Vermeer painted in the 1600s and died when he was 43. "He painted really well but also really slowly," she said. "There are fewer than three dozen of his paintings still around."

"How many is that?" Matt asked.

"Thirty-six," Cecily said oh so helpfully.

Mom told us to sit on the floor and pick a painting and draw it.

Well, two were of ladies reading letters, but I didn't choose them.

Matt picked *The Little Street*, which shows a brick building on a quiet street with ladies sewing and scrubbing. I chose *The Milkmaid*, which is a lady calmly pouring milk into a bowl next to a bread basket while light streams in from the side. I hoped that looking at that calm lady might calm me. And I figured that would be a good thing.

Cecily chose *The Milkmaid* too.

"Great choice," Mom said. "Look how serene she is."

"What I don't get," Dad said, "is how Vermeer could paint such inner peace when he had eleven mouths to feed."

(What *I* don't get is how my father can refer to children as "mouths to feed"!)

"I know," Mom answered. "Poor man, he always had money troubles. He died in debt."

"I thought he was famous," Matt said.

"He became famous long *after* his death," Mom explained. "In fact, he's never been more famous than he is right now. We live in a busy, stressful time, so maybe we *need* his quiet scenes."

Then she told us kids to stay put because she and Dad were going to go look at *The Night Watch* again. "We'll be back in five minutes," Dad said.

Five minutes to look at *one* painting!

Well, we started sketching away and trying to feel Vermeer's inner peace and everything, but after about three seconds, Matt said, "I'm done." Cecily complimented him even though, believe me, Matt's picture was no prizewinner.

Meanwhile, Cecily and I kept sketching and coloring, and for some reason, I felt like we were in a race. Inner **peace** was turning into outer **war**.

I was trying to get my picture right—the light

pouring in from the window and the milk pouring out of the jug and the lady's rosy cheeks and the bread's crackly crust.

I was about to say, "I'm done," but Baby Matt let go of his baby tooth and said, "Cecily, I like how you're doing her dress."

Cecily said, "Thanks," and kept coloring the green, blue, and yellow folds of the milkmaid's dress. So I kept coloring too. I even stood up to see how Vermeer made the folds by using different shades of color and different thicknesses of paint, and I tried doing that even though all I had was pencils.

I was about to say, "I'm done," when Young Mr. Art Critic said, "Cecily, you do skin really well."

She said, "Thanks," and kept shading the milk-maid's smooth strong arms.

I figured as long as Cecily kept sketching, I'd keep sketching too. But I have to admit, I was having a really hard time with the twisty little stream of milk that caught and reflected sunlight.

Well, Mom and Dad finally came back, and Mom said, "Oh Matt, that's wonderful," (when his picture *obviously* stunk) and "Very nice, Melanie," (when mine wasn't just very nice, it was *excellent*).

Then Mom looked at Cecily's picture and said, "Cecily! That is luminous!"

She actually said "luminous"! Mom has never once called any of my pictures luminous!

It made me soooo mad! When I'm with Cecily's mom, I get criticized. When Cecily is with my mom, she gets complimented.

Even Dad complimented Cecily's sketch. "It looks like that jug will never run out," he said. "It looks like that milk will keep flowing forever, just like in the real painting."

I should have kept my big mouth shut (duh duh duh), but I didn't. I couldn't. I said,

"WHY DOESN'T ANYBODY LIKE MY PICTURE? WHY DOESN'T ANYBODY LIKE ME?"

Then I went running out of the room and down the hall and down the steps and down another hall until I found the *toiletten*. When I got there, I went into the door for *damsels-in-distress* and slammed it shut and

128

burst into tears and felt sad and mad and stupid and confused and embarrassed all at the exact same time.

I would tell you what happened next but Dad says we have to go have dinner right this very instant N-O-W.

To be continued—

Terrible Melanie
Who committed a Felony

☞ bedtime at the ~
~ canal house ~

Dear Diary,

We're back and Cecily is reading and Matt is coloring and Mom and Dad are in their room and I'm going to tell you what happened.

This is what happened.

I was in the museum bathroom and I was UPSET!
upset upset upset!

I was also totally utterly alone. For all I knew, no one even had a clue where I was. Plus, I had to pee and I had a wedgie.

Anyway, as I was washing my hands, Mom walked in and said, "Honey, what is going on?"

"I'm washing my hands."

"I mean between you and Cecily."

"Nothing."

"I can see that. I'd like to remind you that she is our guest and—"

"You don't have to remind me of how special she is, Mom. You and Dad already act like you love her more than you love me." (I couldn't believe I said that.)

"For heaven's sake!" Mom said. "We invited Cecily along *because* we love you." Mom put her arms around me but I left mine dangling down. "She's far from home and her mom is sick, and she hasn't even been able to talk to her on the phone yet. Of course we're being nice to her! Maybe even extra nice. That's common courtesy and the right thing to do. Besides, I like Cecily. Don't you want me to like your friends?"

I sort of half nodded and I was thinking about hugging her back when Cecily herself walked in. Mom said, "I'll give you two a few minutes to work this out. I'll be waiting outside with Dad and Matt."

Cecily looked at me as though I should talk first.

So I did. I said, "I thought you didn't like Matt the Brat."

"I don't mind him," she said. "It may be a pain to have a brother all the time, but it's not so bad for a week. It's even kind of fun."

"Fun for you."

"What is your problem, Melanie?"

"My problem is that everybody is acting nice to you and you're acting nice to everybody."

"That's a problem?"

"Yes! You're Little Miss Polite."

"I'm a guest. Guests are supposed to act polite. What do you want me to do? Talk back and act rude?"

"Well, you're not being polite to me."

"What?!"

"You're playing little games with Matt—smelling roses and saying 'HHHGHHHowda HHHGHH-Howda HHHGHHHowda.' You even lent him your stuffed animal! And you laugh at my dad's lame jokes and you talk about art with my mom and—"

"For your information, Melanie, I like games and I like to laugh and I like art. Besides, my mom

131

gave me a big long speech before I left about how I'd better be a good guest and better not leave Matt out. So yes, I'm acting nice. Why is that so hard for you?"

"Because I feel like a fifth wheel!" I turned toward the sink and splashed my face with cold water to hide the tears in my eyes. "I don't care if you're a good *guest*," I said. "I want you to be a good *friend*."

"I want *you* to be a good friend too," Cecily said.

"What's that supposed to mean?"

"When I asked you at the windmill if you were mad, you should have answered right then and there instead of giving me the Silent Treatment and getting even madder. And you're always writing—which I don't mind because that's usually when I play with Matt. But then how can *you* mind when I do play with him? And Melanie, do you really think I *want* to sit next to Matt every single second? Every time he asks, I look up at you hoping you'll say 'No, sit with me,' but you never do, so I sit down because I have no choice."

I suddenly pictured Cecily meeting my eyes in the bus and in the canal bike, and I wished I'd been able to read her mind instead of being all caught up in my own feelings.

"I wasn't giving you the Silent Treatment," I said. "I just didn't feel like talking."

Cecily shrugged.

"And I thought I started writing *after* you and Matt started playing," I added. "Not vice versa."

Cecily shrugged again.

"And I always wanted to sit next to you, but I thought you were mad—"

"To tell you the truth," Cecily interrupted, "today I *was* mad at you for not being nice to me. I *know* you're all freaked out about whether you'll see your precious Hedgehog again. But, Melanie, I happen to have bigger worries." I was about to defend Hedgehog, but then Cecily asked, "On that PG-13 beach, didn't it even *occur* to you that I might be thinking about—"

"Your mom?" I sort of choked out.

Cecily could have said "Bingo!" in a sarcastic voice. But she just nodded. Her lower lip started sticking out and trembling a little. I was afraid she might cry. Cecily hardly ever cries. I cry way more

133

than she does and I don't cry all that much (not as much as Matt anyway).

"I'm sorry," I said because I could see her point. I really hadn't looked at things her way, only my way. I'd been acting like a horse with blinders on. I'd been worried about whether Cecily and Mrs. Hausner were mad at me, when they were worried about much bigger things. In fact, maybe Cecily *has* been thinking about life-and-death stuff all vacation. "Your mom is going to be all right," I said. "And you'll get to talk to her soon." Cecily half nodded, but I could tell she was holding back tears.

"I wish she didn't need an operation at all," Cecily said.

"I know." I gave her a hug.

Just then Mom came in. "C'mon, girls," she said, "Dad's getting antsy. Are you ready to look at doll-houses from the 1600s?"

"*Dollhouses?!*" I said. "Give us a break!" I looked at Cecily and rolled my eyes.

She rolled her eyes back and we went and looked at the museum's fancy collection of dollhouses.

They were awesome, like mini-mansions! We had to climb up wooden steps just to peek inside and see the rooms decorated with carved furniture, silk wallpaper, marble floors, and woven rugs. The beds and chairs all looked real, but shrunken. "These must have taken forever to build," I said, and Cecily said, "The kids must have loved them." We started talking about how we used to give our dolls toothpaste shampoos. And then we kept on talking talking talking.

We are now getting ready for bed. Matt just asked Cecily what kind of pillow she likes best. "The hard kind that holds your head up or the soft kind that lets you sink into a land of feathers?"

Cecily said, "I like both." She smiled at me and threw her pillow at Matt.

"Missed me!" he said and threw it back at her.

We were about to have a big pillow fight (which is way more fun than having a fight-fight) but Mom came in and said, "Night-night! Sleep tight! Don't let the bed bugs bite!"

"Bugs?" Matt said.

"Go to sleep!" Mom said.

I was going to write-write a fight-fight night-night poem but

I'm way too tired
To be inspired.

Sleepily yours,
Merry Mellie

August 16
very early morning in the canal house

Dear Diary,

Mom and Dad still haven't come in saying "Rise and shine!" so Cecily and Matt are playing cards (Spit and Bloody Knuckles).

In some ways, Amsterdam is a lot like New York—or New Amsterdam! Both are big cities with split personalities. You could say they are beautiful and artsy or dirty and grimy and either way, you'd be right. When it comes to food, both have all kinds of different restaurants: French, Italian, Mexican, Chinese, Japanese, Greek, Turkish, Indian, you name it!

Last night, we went to an Indian restaurant with

Indian music and Indian incense. Matt ordered a mango drink, Cecily ordered a papaya drink, and Mom and Dad ordered "a couple of Heinies." I ordered regular water, no bubbles.

Dad started going on and on about how fresh the beer tastes in Holland and how if we were older, we could all tour the Heineken brewery and learn how beer is made. I said, "Daaad!" and he stopped. Even when I'm a grown-up, I will never like beer. It smells sour and probably tastes worse than it smells, and some people drink too much of it and get big beer bellies. (Even if I did like beer, I would still never ask for a "Heinie"!!)

Everyone ordered a lot of weird food, and Matt and I ordered lamb. The lamb was completely smothered in spinach sauce, which I didn't like, so I kept wiping it off with my napkin. Matt didn't like the sauce either, so he kept dipping his lamb bites into his water glass and stirring until his lamb came out squeaky clean.

Well, Mom suddenly noticed our sauce-removal techniques and was *totally* grossed out and horrified. "Where are your table manners?" she asked, and started fussing at us. (At least she didn't add, "You don't see

Cecily using her napkin as a washcloth or her water glass as a sink.") When she was all done scolding us, Mom said, "Who raised you kids?" which showed that at least she had a tiny speck of a sense of humor about the whole thing. Then she reminded Matt to stay away from hot and spicy sauces.

I separated the yummies from the yuckies on my plate, but I did *not* do any food transfers.

Back at the canal house, Hendrik said our luggage still had not arrived!

At least we have new pajamas and clean underwear.

We got in our pj's, and Matt, instead of doing his usual rush-brush, was holding his toothbrush still and moving his face from side to side. He showed Cecily his sickeningly wiggly tooth. He even showed her a little lamb chunk he flossed out from between his back teeth. He is inventing a new game called Disgusting Discoveries: Whoever flosses out the biggest thing wins.

"*Ewww!!*" Cecily said. "I'm sorry, Matt, but I don't want to play Floss Show-and-Tell or whatever you call it!" She might be finally finding out that having a brother full-time even for a few days has serious downsides.

"Hate to break it to you, Newt Brain," I said. "But face it: You are a major dork." Matt stuck out his tongue at me, so I added, "I should know because I'm older."

"You *are* older," Matt agreed, "and that just means you're going to die first."

"Does not!" I was about to pummel him when Dad walked in.

"Lights out," Dad said and within about two minutes, Matt started breathing all evenly, DogDog or no DogDog.

For a few minutes, our room was really quiet.

Then Cecily whispered, "Mel, are you asleep?"

I almost almost almost was, but I was so glad we were friends again that I whispered, "No."

"When my mom first told me she had cancer, she tried to make it sound like it was no big deal," Cecily said. "But then everyone started phoning and sending cards and stopping by, so I knew it *was* a big deal. And now the thing I'm worried about most is that my grand-mom died of breast cancer."

I didn't know what to say, but finally I asked, "Did you know her?"

"Yes. Her name was Florence—my middle name—and she died when I turned five."

"Was she nice?"

"Really nice. She always wore bangly bracelets and the tops of her arms were all jiggly and flappy and soft. You know?"

I nodded, but then I realized it was pitch-black in our room, so I said, "I know what you mean."

"Whenever she came to visit," Cecily said, "she brought homemade brownies."

I was so tired, I think I started dozing and half dreaming about chocolatey brownies. But when I heard Cecily say, "I also remember that—" I turned and propped myself on my elbow. "—Grandmom Flo had a really nice laugh," Cecily continued. "When she laughed, you felt really happy, and you tried to say or do something that would make her laugh again."

"What was it like when she died?"

"Sometimes my mom would cry in the middle of washing dishes or listening to the radio or when I didn't expect it."

"I wish I could have met your grandmom," I said. "But it's good you have her middle name."

"It's old-fashioned, but I like it."

"And it's good you have her laugh."

"What do you mean?"

"Your laugh makes people happy too."

"You think so?"

"I know so. And you know what else is good?"

"What?"

"It's good that medicines are better today than they used to be and doctors know more." I was glad it occurred to me to say that. Cecily probably was too. She didn't say anything, though, so I added, "My mom told me that a lot of women get breast cancer, but *not* so many die of it. She said most women get better because nowadays doctors usually find out about it early enough to, you know, fix it."

Cecily stayed quiet but I knew she was awake. Then she said, "The operation is tomorrow morning—which I guess means tomorrow afternoon here."

"Your mom will be okay," I said. "Don't worry." (I can't believe *I* told *Cecily* not to worry!)

"Thanks," she mumbled.

She didn't say anything after that and I was wondering if she was upset because I heard her make a snuffly sound. But then I heard her breathing as evenly as Matt the Brat and I realized she was fast asleep.

WiTh ♡ From HoLLand

Melanie

P.S. I'm crossing my fingers for Mrs. Hausner! Before bed, Mom took me aside and said that tomorrow we'll have to think positive and stay busy.

in the Bej Begijnhof
(Ba Hhhain Hof) courtyard

Dear Diary,

At 9:30 A.M. Holland time, our luggage *still* hadn't come. Dad called, and the man said they were "searching it right now."

"I thought you've *been* searching for it!" Dad said. The man explained that they were *searching it* not *searching for it*—in other words, they found our luggage and it's going through customs! So now they will deliver it to us very soon.

HURRAY!

If and when it truly comes, I'll write hip hip hurray!!

When Hedgehog gets here,
I will Cheer Cheer Cheer!!!

All we kids really wanted to do was stay inside and wait for our stuff. But Dad said he was starving, so he dragged us out for a breakfast buffet. Next thing you know, he and Mom were eating salmon and herring and cheeses and Matt was having a ham sandwich—for breakfast! Cecily and I just had fruit salad and pastries. There were also little boxes of chocolate sprinkles on the buffet table, so Matt made himself a sprinkle sandwich for dessert, and Cecily and I sprinkled sprinkles on our hot chocolate.

We were talking about middle names, and Cecily said, "My grandmother was named Florence and my grandfather was named Lawrence, but nobody called them Florence and Lawrence. Everyone called them Flo and Lo."

Mom and Dad laughed and I did too.

Matt went to the *toiletten*, and when he came back, he announced, "I have toilet paper on my shoe."

Cecily said, "Here, let me step on it and get it off for you."

"No!" Matt said. "I like it!" He started walking around our table with a bright white half-square of t.p. trailing behind him.

Ordinarily, I would have told him not to be an idiot. But I was so happy that Cecily and I made up and that our luggage got found that instead of calling Matt an idiot, I said, "Go faster!"

Matt started circling the table faster and faster and faster, and Cecily and I started laughing and laughing.

Dad said, "Sit down this instant, young man!"

Mom said, "Children, you are being very disruptive!"

Matt sat down but he peeked up at us and Cecily winked and I had to bite my lip to stop laughing.

Dad looked really annoyed (hee hee), so, probably to get back on his good side, Matt picked up a sign on our table and asked, "What's this?" The sign had a yin-yang with a cigarette and a rambling paragraph in

English and Dutch about "harmony and mutual respect" and how it's quite all right to smoke, just not right here.

Personally, I do NOT think it's quite all right to smoke and I do NOT think yin-yangs and cigarettes belong together! I even said so. Dad agreed, but he said the Dutch pride themselves on being tolerant. They actually have coffee shops just for smokers!

"What's tolerant?" Matt asked.

"Tolerant is having respect for other people and accepting their differences. You know about the Pilgrims, right?"

Cecily and I both nodded, but I was thinking that I might have forgotten whatever I was supposed to know. Matt said, "What about them?"

"Long ago in England, everyone was forced to join the Church of England. Some people said, 'No way!' and left. They were the Pilgrims. Guess where they went?"

"Where???" Matt asked, as though nothing could be more fascinating.

"Here! To Holland—the little country with the big history."

"Why???" He glanced at me and I had to keep biting my lip.

"Because they knew no one would boss them around or discriminate just because their religion was different. They would be welcomed and accepted." I could feel a full-fledged Dad lecture coming on. Once, Dad went on and on about politics on the walk to school, and I was about to fall asleep standing up, but then that very day, Miss Sands asked if anyone could name both our state's U.S. senators and I raised my hand and everybody looked at me like I was this amazing genius (even Norbert, who was new in school).

"Follow me," Dad said. "I'm going to show you a place that's frozen in time." I think he and Mom mostly wanted us to be outside before we got disruptive again.

We followed Dad down a few streets, being careful not to get run over by bicyclists. Matt was walking extra slowly so the t.p. on his shoe wouldn't fall off, but it fell off anyway. When we reached an old arched doorway, Dad said, "Close your eyes."

"This is like No Peeking!" Matt said.

"When you open your eyes," Dad said, "you will

walk through this door and feel like you're stepping into another world. Ready? Open your eyes!"

Well, we walked into a courtyard and it was green and pretty and tranquil (as Mom put it) and had old houses with fancy gabled roofs. But it did *not* look "frozen in time." It was hundreds of years old, not millions. And it's not as if there were cavemen running around in loincloths or anything.

"See that church?" Dad asked. "The Pilgrims prayed in peace right there—*before* sailing across the ocean."

Matt was wiggling his tooth all around, but I could tell that now he was listening for real. "Did they make it across?"

Even I knew the answer to that one!

"It took two months and it was very rough. One person died and another was born," Dad said. "But in 1620, a hundred and two Pilgrims landed in what is now Massachusetts."

"On the *Mayflower*," Mom added. "You've heard of the *Mayflower*," she said, and squeezed Matt's angelic little hand.

Matt took that as his cue to tell his second-favorite

147

joke (after the pea soup joke). He asked Cecily, "If April showers bring May flowers, what do Mayflowers bring?"

"June bugs?" Cecily said just to be nice.

"Pilgrims!" Matt said, all proud of himself.

Dad and Mom exchanged a Matt-is-precious smile.

Cecily and I exchanged a Matt-is-dorky smile.

"The Pilgrims started the Plimoth Plantation," Dad said.

"My dad took me," Cecily said. "It's where they had the first Thanksgiving. They ate with spoons, not forks."

"Cool," Matt said.

"Meanwhile, to the south," Dad droned, "a Dutchman named Peter Minuit was tying up a little real-estate deal—he bought the island of Manhattan for twenty-four bucks! Some say he paid more; some say the Native Americans never thought of it as *selling* Mother Earth—"

Matt yawned. "Can I run around?"

Mom said, "Sure," and Matt scampered off like an American squirrel.

Cecily and I wandered off too. Mom said that nuns used to live around here, so Cecily and I tried to pretend we were nuns. We walked along with our eyes cast down and our hearts full of goodness. But then one of us would look at the other and we'd both burst out giggling.

After a while, Matt said, "Cecily, let's play Pencil Portraits." So now I'm writing and they're drawing. Cecily's picture of Matt is about a bazillion times better than Matt's of Cecily. (If I were Cecily, I'd be insulted.)

Dad's telling Mom about an opera called *The Flying Dutchman*. It's about a doomed ship's captain who gets stuck far out at sea. It sounds like he'll never ever get to go home. Ever.

"Does it have a happy ending?" I asked.

"No," Dad said. "But some operas do. One of these days, I'll take you to the Met."

"And I'll take you to the Frick," Mom said, "so you can see my favorite Rembrandt."

I considered saying "Goody goody gumdrops," but didn't.

Mom said, "How about if right now I take all of you to a wax museum?"

"Wax?" Matt said. "Who cares about wax? We already learned about cheese."

I was about to agree that we couldn't care less about candles, but Mom said it's not a museum *about* wax, it's a museum of people *made* of wax.

"You're going to love it," Mom said.

"I went to the one in New York," Cecily said. "It has George Washington and Helen Keller and Whoopi Goldberg. It was fun but sort of scary too."

"Like how?" Matt asked.

"Like Marie Antoinette's head gets chopped off over and over and over again."

"Awesome!" Matt said.

Well, we are going to the wax museum. I have no idea *what* to expect. But I'll tell you this: If it stinks, I'm going to be mad.

TOLERANTLY YOURS,
MUSEUM MEL

late lunch at a pancake restaurant

Dear Diary,

It didn't STINK!

Madame Tussaud's is the **funnest** museum I've ever ever ever been to! In fact, I think all museums should be wax museums!

You pronounce it Mad Am To Sew. Everyone in it (except the tourists) is made of wax. You know how Michelangelo sculptures are made of marble? Well, these sculptures are made of wax! And some of them look totally alive! There's a wax Oprah, wax Einstein, wax Gandhi, wax Winston Churchill, wax Martin Luther King, and a wax Pope. Matt loved a spooky scene of two upside-down dead guys with wax blood dribbling out of them. (He kept saying "Awesome!" but also kept clinging on to Mom for dear life.)

The museum takes you on a history tour, starting from when Spain ruled Holland through the Golden Age, when Rembrandt and Vermeer were painting like crazy and Amsterdam was the world's richest and most free city. (Is "freest" a word? "Freeest" can't be.)

Anyway, it was pretty cool to be walking among so many famous people. Dad took a picture of Mom blowing kisses to Vincent van Gogh and of me curtsying before Beatrix, Queen of the Netherlands.

Matt tried an experiment. He tried to stand perfectly still to see if anyone would think he was a famous wax boy and take a picture of him. Well, Matt can't freeze for even two seconds, so—big surprise—nobody even paused. He did not fool a single solitary person!

Cecily said she liked this museum more than the one in New York.

At the gift shop, I bought a postcard of Anne Frank. Cecily bought a postcard of Mel Gibson for her mom, and my mom gave her shoulder a squeeze and smiled at her in a serious sort of way. I saw a postcard of Tina Turner in fishnet stockings and a leather bathing suit, so I said half jokingly, "We should send this to Christopher and sign it 'Your secret admirers.'"

Cecily laughed. "We should. Let's."

"It would have a Dutch stamp on it. He'd know it was from us."

"Then forget it—no way!"

I have to say: It's way more fun to laugh with Cecily than to watch her laugh with everyone else! (But I wonder if deep down she's feeling extra worried right now. When I think about it, she *was* a little quiet at the museum.)

I showed her my latest poem:

> The people made of wax
> Help teach us lots of facts.
> We learn about the Dutch
> And like them very much.
> (Too bad the signs say DO NOT TOUCH.)

Outside Madame Tussaud's is a big square called the Dam (pronounced Dom, *not* you-know-how). We saw a statue of a knight in shining armor. You couldn't tell if it was made of wax or metal or what, so Matt marched up to the knight statue, and it . . . moved! It was alive!! It patted Matt on the head!!!

Matt jumped about a foot (hee hee) and Dad snapped

a picture and Mom gave the man a few coins. That's what we do in New York when someone on the street plays music or does something artistic.

Suddenly, it started drizzling, so we had to find a restaurant.

On the way, though, I almost lost my appetite because we saw a little boy eat raw fish. Right in the street! His dad held a fish by the tail and lowered it right into the little boy's mouth and the boy ate it!

Gross! Yuck! Ewww!

Dad said it's a Dutch tradition and he'd be happy to buy us some herring.

I said, "In your dreams."

Matt said, "No way, José."

Cecily said, "No, thank you." (Even she is not thaaaat good at trying new foods!)

Dad said the Dutch say: "A herring a day keeps the doctor away."

I said, "Forget it."

Matt said, "We're not Dutch."

Cecily said, "No, thank you," again.

We did end up eating a fast lunch of pancakes or

pannekoeken (Panna Coook Ahn). Yum yum yum. And now it has stopped raining, so we're finally going back to the canal house, where our luggage should be by now.

Hang in there, Hedgehog. I'm on my way!

Bestest,
   Mama Mellie

                                   afternoon at the canal house

Dear Diary,

HiP HiP HuRRAY!!!

Hendrik, the check-in man, who is chubby if I may be perfectly honest, has been acting like Mr. Busy whenever he sees us. I think he's been trying to avoid us because we always ask about our luggage when it's not his fault it got so lost.

Well guess what? This time he said, "I have good news for you," only it sounded like "I hof gooood noose."

Mom said, "Did our luggage come?"

"Yes," he said, and pointed to a pile of stuff—all ours!

Matt started jumping up and down and I went right up to my duffle and unzipped it and reached in and pulled out Hedgehog.

I looked into her brown eyes and kissed her pink snout and petted her soft stick-uppy fur. She is even sweeeeter and cuuuuter than I'd been picturing. She was probably as happy to see me as I was to see her. I could almost swear she licked my nose (even though I know that's impossible).

I also yanked out DogDog and tossed him to Matt and he started dancing around in a half-cute, half-dorky way.

Now we are all upstairs and our animals are on our pillows and our clothes are put away except for the clean ones we changed into. I put on my blue jeans and my soft pink sweater.

We would probably be celebrating except that the chubby check-in man handed Mom and Dad a note. It said that Cecily's dad had called from the hospital. But there was no message. The note just said that he called—not that her mom is okay.

Poor Cecily! She read the piece of paper over and over and tears started shining in her eyes. She really wants to talk to her parents! And I don't blame her.

Even though her parents are divorced, they act like friends. I once asked Cecily if she thought there was a chance they'd ever get remarried and she said, "Zero." Still, it's good her dad is taking care of her mom while we're taking care of Cecily.

The operation was this morning and Cecily said that when her mom leaves the hospital, she'll have to rest a lot. She won't be allowed to drive or carry things or exercise or shower or anything. Cecily also told me something that is hard to imagine. She said the doctors are supposed to take *off* one of her mom's breasts and build *on* a new one.

Cecily and I used to pull out our Barbies' arms and legs and even pop out their heads before putting them all back together again. But it's hard to picture doctors taking off and putting on parts of real people.

Right this second, Cecily is trying to call America. Unfortunately the hospital-room phone number is busy

busy busy. Mom said her mom must have taken the phone off the hook so she could get some rest. Cecily tried the hospital's main number, but the lady couldn't give out any information. Cecily left a message that said, "I love you. Please call back."

Mom said she was sure Cecily's mom was going to be fine.

Cecily said she has a stomach ache.

Yours—

Melanie AND Hedgehog

P.S. If I were Cecily, I'd have a stomach ache too. What if her dad was calling with bad news???

2 hours later

Dear Diary,

It's rainy out, so we're staying in. (I think we're really staying in so we'll be here if Cecily's parents call.)

I'm glad we're inside, but I don't mind rain because I like twirling my umbrella and making the raindrops go flying and I also like how clean it smells after a rain, like Mother Nature has given the world a shower.

Mom just showed us a very cool book of a Dutch artist named M. C. Escher who was born in 1898. When you look at his illustrations, first you see one thing, then you see something completely different. He drew one picture of white birds flying right, but it's also a picture of black birds flying left! He also drew staircases that seem to be leading you up—but also leading you down. Mom said that there are many ways of seeing things and that the more you look, the more you see.

When I'm reading Anne Frank's diary, I see the world the way she saw it. And when I look at a painting, I see the world the way the painter saw it. It's almost like trying on someone else's glasses or point of view.

Here is what I've been thinking: If Cecily kept a diary of this very same vacation, it would be really different from my diary.

I was also thinking it was pretty dumb of me not to realize that one reason Cecily has been telling us "Don't worry" every two seconds is probably because *she* is worried out of her mind.

When we get back home, I wonder if she'll be able to give her mom a big bear hug. Maybe it will have to be a gentle little snuggle.

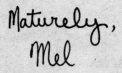

Maturely,
Mel

a little later

Dear Diary,

While Cecily was in the bathroom, Matt the Brat asked me what everyone is tense about and if Cecily was my "bosom buddy" and if her mom has "a boo-boo on her booby." (For a little kid, he has big ears!)

I said, "Matt, that is not funny. Don't be childish."

"But I'm a child."

"Then don't be babyish."

"But I'm a baby."

"Just be more sensitive."

"What's *sensitive?*" he asked.

I said, "Sensitive is when you think about other people's feelings, not just your own."

He said, "What do you mean?"

I said, "Just be nice to Cecily, okay?"

He said, "I'm always nice to Cecily," which, I have to admit, is true.

Sensitively yours,
Melanie

Dear Diary,

YAY! Cecily got to talk to her dad! Mom talked to him too. Cecily's mom was still too "out of it" to get on the phone. I don't know if that means she was groggy from pain pills or from anesthesia. (It makes you go into a deep fake sleep.)

When Cecily got to talk to her dad, she had tears in her eyes again. But they were the happy kind. She seems really relieved.

I am too.

Dad and Matt went out to get Dutch sandwiches and raisin rolls, so Mom invited Cecily and me into her room. She patted the bed, and Cecily and I sat down. I thought Mom was going to deal out a game of Concentration, but she said that since it was just us girls, it was a good opportunity to talk. "Cecily, your mom's doing great," Mom said. "And your dad asked me to help answer any questions you have. Okay?"

Cecily said she doesn't completely understand what's going on, and it would help if Mom explained everything from the start.

So Mom began. She said that after Cecily's mom found that little lump in her breast, she made a doctor's appointment and an x-ray appointment, and then a doctor used a needle to take out a tiny piece of the lump and test it. Unfortunately, the test showed that she had cancer. Fortunately, the cancer had not spread. The doctors even checked her armpits (P.U.!) and all around but the cancer seemed to be contained in one place. (Mom didn't say P.U., of course—*I* threw that in.)

What Mom did say was that many women who have breast cancer ask the doctors to cut out just the lump. Then the women usually have treatments (like radiation, which is light beams, or chemotherapy, which is chemicals) to make sure no cancer gets left behind.

Since Cecily's mom's mom had also had breast cancer, Cecily's mom and the different doctors decided that in her case, the best way to get rid of the cancer would be to take away the breast once and for all. That's called a mastectomy, and it's not what everybody decides to do, but it's what Cecily's mom decided to do.

Cecily winced like she'd been pinched and Mom

said, "I know this is hard to hear, but your mom is a strong woman, and the surgery was successful."

Mom also said that Cecily's mom wanted to get the whole thing over with. "She'll still get check-ups—all women do—but chances are excellent that the cancer is completely gone. She got rid of it. Your dad said the surgery went very well and it looks like she won't even need any extra treatments. Just bed rest."

"Can kids get breast cancer?" I asked.

"No," Mom said.

"What about the new breast?" Cecily asked. I was glad she could talk to my mom. I even felt proud of my mom for being the easy-to-talk-to kind.

"Different doctors built a matching new breast right on her," Mom said. "Once she's all healed up, no one will even know what she went through."

Cecily asked, "Do you think it hurt?" Tears spilled out of her eyes.

Mom hugged her and said, "The doctors gave your mom painkillers."

Then Cecily asked, "Where did they get the extra skin for the new breast?"

"From your mother's own tummy," Mom said. "So she didn't just have breast surgery—she had a tummy tuck too!"

"She wasn't fat," I said.

"Not at all," Mom agreed. "She's always looked great and she always will. She'll probably look the same as ever."

I wonder if that could be true.

"I'm glad the operation is over—the take-away part and the build-on part," Cecily said. "You really think my mom is going to be okay?"

"I really think so," Mom said, and gave her another hug.

I way dying to ask, "Are you sure *you* are okay?" but decided it would be more sensitive to ask later.

Besides, by then, Dad and Matt had come back with the sandwiches and a bottle of water for the kids and a bottle of wine for the grown-ups.

Well, we were all B.P.s (oink oink) and we ate every crumb and and drank every drop.

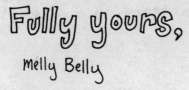

Fully yours,
melly Belly

on a bench in Vondelpark

Dear Diary,

It's funny how Dutch is a tiny bit like English but also not at all like English—depending on how you look at it.

Dad's guidebook says bread is *brood* (Brrode) and butter is *boter* (Bow Ter). Cabbage is *kool* (Kole) and sausage is *worst* (Vorst). Liver is *lever* (Layv Er), which is easy to remember, but who would ever want to order *lever*???

Dad taught us to count to three in Dutch:

1 *een* (Ayn)

2 *twee* (Tway)

3 *drie* (Dree)

When you are in a foreign land,
It's fun to try to understand
The language that the people speak—
But what can you learn in a week?

I may not be learning much Dutch (much Dutch—that's a rhyme!), but I'm learning other stuff. For instance, Amsterdam is farther north than New York City, so it stays light outside until very late, which means our summer vacation days last extraaaa loooonnng.

Well, Mom wanted to spend *all day* at the Van Gogh Museum, so Dad said he'd take us for a bike ride and picnic and we'd meet her there later.

Instead of buying picnic food at a big supermarket, like in America, we bought cheese at a cheese shop, fruit at a fruit shop, and bread at a bread shop, and we each took turns paying.

We also bought a box of chocolates. Matt asked Dad, "Can I have one?"

"Not before lunch."

"Can I poke a hole in one?"

"Absolutely not."

"But don't you want to know what's inside?"

"I'm a grown-up," Dad said. "I can wait."

At the picnic, Matt was chomping on his sandwich and wiggling his tooth. He said that he could push his tooth way over with his tongue so that the top of the tooth faced sideways. (Gross!) Then he asked, "Can you stick out your tongue and touch your nose?" All of us, even Dad, tried to touch our noses with our tongues (it must have looked pretty dorky). But none of us could do it. Then Matt said, "I can!" and he stuck out his tongue and touched his nose—*with his finger.*

I didn't know whether to laugh or punch him, but then he said, "My tooth fell out! My tooth fell out!"—only it sounded more like "My toof fell out! My toof fell out!"

A teeny drop of saliva splashed on me, so I said, "Say it, don't spray it. I want the news, not the weather."

"That *is* the news," Matt answered. "I lost my first tooth!" He held it high and smiled a smile with a hole in it.

Cecily said, "Put it someplace safe so you don't lose it twice!" He stuck the tooth in his pants pocket and she gave him a high five. Dad did too. So I did too.

CU,
melanie

on a bench in the Van Gogh museum

Dear Diary,

Mom noticed the hole in Matt's smile right away, and Matt told her all about it, beaming away as if he were the first person in the history of the world to lose a tooth. Then Mom told all three of us to tie our shoes, and said she doesn't understand why shoelace makers can't make shoelaces that stay tied. She always says that. She says that if we can make rockets that go to other planets, we should be able to make shoelaces that stay tied.

The Van Gogh Museum has over two hundred paintings, five hundred sketches, and seven hundred letters, and Mom said she was going to give us a guided tour. I was worried it was going to be a snooze, but since Mom is so into van Gogh, I decided to act interested. Well guess what? Vincent van Gogh's life was interesting, and his paintings are really really really good. We even got to see the paintings of sunflowers and irises that we had pieced together as puzzles.

Here's the thing. If you step back, you see the subject

that van Gogh painted, but if you step up close, you see a jumble of different colors. For example, when he painted his own skin, he didn't paint it just skin color. He used green, red, blue, yellow, black, and white. He saw things in lots of ways—depending on the time of day and on how he was feeling—which was often mixed-up and shaky, just like his colors and brush strokes. Some of his paintings actually seem to be moving. Stars twinkle and clouds swirl and flowers bloom or droop right before your very eyes.

Unlike Vermeer's, van Gogh's paintings are *not* calm.

I've been thinking: maybe my life is like a van Gogh painting. If I look at it up close, things sometimes seem not quite right. But if I step back a little, things usually seem pretty good!

It is soooo pitiful that he sold only one painting and died at age 37. He didn't really even start painting until he was 27! I wish he'd sold bunches and kept on painting for years.

By the way, the Dutch don't pronounce his name van Go. They say van Goff or van Hoff with that

HHHGHHH gargly sound they all make. So if you were making a rhyme, you wouldn't say "Van Go was psycho," you'd say "Life was rough for van Hoff."

Here's a poem I wrote:

Van Gogh spent hours
Painting sunflowers.
He also liked drawing
Crows flying and cawing.
People thought his work was bad.
I think that is sad sad sad.

Today everyone loves his paintings and they sell for bazillions of dollars. A portrait he did of his doctor sold for $82,500,000—the most money anyone had ever spent on a painting. When van Gogh was alive, though, nobody appreciated him. It was as if he was a big loser. Even *he* didn't always appreciate his work— he didn't even sign most of his paintings!

The only person who was nice to him was his little brother Theo. Theo had an art gallery in Paris and tried really hard to sell Vincent's paintings, but no one wanted them. Theo sent Vincent money anyway because Vincent needed it and Theo loved him. Later, when Theo and his wife had a baby boy, they named him Vincent.

If Matt ever had a daughter, I wonder if he'd name her Melanie.

Anyway, poor Vincent van Gogh ended up going crazy. He had a fight with a painter named Paul Gauguin, and Vincent cut off his own ear. Not the whole thing, but part of it. Some people think he did it because he said that no one liked him because he was a bad listener, so what did he need his ear for? But really he did it because he was mentally ill. Mom showed us a self-portrait with a big bandage around his head. Even though van Gogh ended up going to a mental hospital, he kept painting really fast and really well. Then in 1890, he shot himself in a wheat field. He killed himself—but it took him TWO DAYS to die!

Six months after that, his brother Theo died too. Mom said, "Some say he died of a broken heart," but Dad said, "Nonsense! He died of syphilis." That's a disease.

The van Gogh brothers are buried side by side in

France, where they moved when they left Holland. Mom once visited their graves. She said maybe she'd take us there someday.

If you ask me, the best van Gogh paintings are his self-portraits and old shoes. I also like a really creepy one of a skull with a lit cigarette in its bony mouth! Mom thinks the American Cancer Society should use it to help teenagers not smoke. I told her to get a poster for her classroom and she thought that was a good idea.

"When van Gogh was alive," Matt asked, "did he ever visit that other museum we went to?"

Mom ate up that question. She said van Gogh liked the Rijksmuseum and admired Rembrandt's work.

"They were both really good at self-portraits," I said.

"The best!" Mom agreed. She said that one reason van Gogh painted himself so often was because he wanted to learn to paint portraits but he couldn't afford to pay models. He was so poor that sometimes he painted on *both* sides of a canvas just to save money on art supplies.

What amazes me is how nice Theo was to his brother. I can't imagine Matt working hard to send me money, or me working hard to send Matt money!

I wonder if Theo and Vincent fought when they were kids.

Right now Matt is next to me on a bench, blowing on his arm making little farty noises. He's making them quietly so Dad doesn't get mad. Matt is also whisper-singing, "Oh where, oh where did van Gogh go? Oh where, oh where did he go go go?" He's trying to make us laugh and it's half working because Cecily is laughing and I'm trying not to.

The problem with Matt is that he acts his age, which, unfortunately, is six and a half. Sometimes he acts like he's six going on two. Mom should yell at him more. If he were my kid, I'd give him a permanent time-out until he was seven at least.

I told Cecily that in Italy, our favorite museum game was Point Out the Naked People, and Mom never even minded so long as we were paying attention to art. Italy has more nudie paintings than Holland, though. That might be because many Italian painters painted naked gods, goddesses, and Bible people, while van Gogh, for instance, painted real people—farmers and postmen and himself. (And you don't see too many real people

174

running around naked, do you? Except maybe at certain beaches!)

The museum game we're playing now is called Find a Bench and Sit Down Quick. Mom does *not* approve. She said, "How can you be more excited about sitting down than seeing paintings?"

Sometimes Mom just doesn't get it.

Signed,

Melanie, A Culture Vulture with tired wings.

at a restaurant (it's taking forever to pay)

7:30 P.M.

Dear Diary,

Guess what happened before we left the Van Gogh Museum? I went to the *Dames* room and I was washing my hands, and a gold ring was just sitting by the faucet. I didn't want it to fall down the drain, so I put it on. It looked pretty good, but I could imagine the conversation I would end up having with Mom if I wore it out:

Mom: "Where did you get this?"

Me: "In the bathroom. It's pretty, isn't it?"

Mom: "Very. But it isn't yours."

Me: "Someone left it. Look, it fits."

Mom: "That's not the point."

Me: "If I don't take it, somebody else will."

Mom: "Not if we turn it in at the Lost and Found."

I thought about it and figured I might as well slide the ring off my finger. So I did. Then I went outside and said, "Do you think this place has a Lost and Found?"

Well, we went there and the man took my ring as though it were nothing, as though I weren't making a personal sacrifice. He was all business, and at first I was half wishing I'd buried the ring in my pocket and ignored my dumb conscience. Finders keepers, losers weepers.

Then a young woman came flying over, all upset and frantic. She started talking a mile a minute in French, and she said she'd left her ring in the bathroom (Mom translated). The Dutchman handed her the ring and pointed to little old me. Well, she was soooo happy, she kissed me on both cheeks and said, *"Merci merci merci"* (Mare Sea Mare Sea Mare Sea), and explained in French that the ring had been a gift from her *grand-père* (Grahn Pear), or grandfather. Then she thanked me one more time and dashed off.

Dad said, "Cupcake, you made her day."

Mom just smiled.

Bestest,

late late late

Dear Diary,

When we got back from dinner, the phone rang. I answered. It was Cecily's mom! Her voice sounded very quiet and faraway and she said, "Hello, Melanie, this is Mrs. Hausner." I didn't say anything. I just handed the phone over to Cecily. Afterward I realized I should have said, "Hello, Mrs. Hausner," or "How are you?" or *something*.

I still feel bad that I hung up on her back when she was crabby and I didn't know why. I also feel bad that I haven't said a word to her about being sick. When I came back from Italy with stitches in my eyebrow, Mrs. Hausner asked all about it.

Cecily is really happy now, and I'm happy for her. She said her mom told her that she is fine and that Cheshire Cat and Honey Bunny are fine too. "But you know what, Mel?" Cecily said. "I'd almost forgotten about them! When I'm at my dad's, I usually ask Mom about them, but this time, I didn't even think about Chesh or Hon-Bun. That's how worried I've been about my mom."

"I bet you're relieved now."

"You can say that again," Cecily said.

"I bet you're relieved now," I said again, and Cecily called me a dork, and we both laughed because I knew she was kidding.

"Cecily," I said, "I know you're a private person and everything, but if you're ever really worried, you should tell me because I don't think I'm all that great at mind reading."

"Okay," Cecily said.

"Really," I said. "I feel kind of bad that when we first got here, I wasn't, you know, more sensitive."

"Don't worry," she said, and I was actually glad that she said, "Don't worry."

"You should tell me little stuff too," I said. "Even no-big-deal stuff. Like when you got Caller I.D." Then I thought that it wasn't exactly Cecily's fault that I kept hanging up on her mom, so I added, "And I'll try harder to listen better."

Cecily nodded and yawned and went to brush her teeth.

Believe it or not, Mom and Dad and Matt are *already* fast asleep.

Right before going to bed, Matt said that brushing his teeth was extra easy because he doesn't have as many as usual.

Pleasant Dreamszzzzz

Mel

Dear Diary,

OH NO!

Cecily is brushing her teeth and I just heard her spitting, and it suddenly dawned on me that every single one of us forgot about Matt's tooth!!!

What about the tooth fairy??? Do they even have tooth fairies in Holland? Or Dutch dwarves??! Did Matt remember to put his tooth under his pillow?

I just checked.

Matt remembered.

Oh God, I mean gosh.

His tooth is *sitting* there.

Ready and waiting for action.

This is TERRIBLE!

Why?

Because if there is no tooth fairy in Holland, that would be hard for Matt to take. Can you imagine being six and a half and putting your tooth under your pillow and finding it still there the next morning? That would stink!

I have to do something. But what???

Mission accomplished!

I searched all my pockets and stuck all my coins under Matt's pillow. I don't even know how much money I jammed in there. I had a euro, which is the coin that works all around Europe. And I had a tiny old guilder and two dimes and one quarter. While I was shoving it all under Matt's head, he snuffled and mumbled something in a foreign language. Maybe Dutch! But he did not wake up.

I, Melanie Martin, just saved the day. Or night. Or morning.

Yay me! I feel kind of like that make-believe Dutch boy who poked his finger in the dike and stopped the flood.

PROUDLY YOURS,
Melanie the P.B.S.

August 18

dawn probably

Dear Diary,

Matt woke us up way early because he was soooo excited that the tooth fairy found him all the way in Amster Amster Dam Dam Dam.

He showed us all his loot, and under his pillow, along with all the coins, there was a crisp American dollar bill! And his tooth was *nowhere* to be seen!

I for one did *not* take away his tooth. Mostly because it didn't occur to me. Even if it had, I wouldn't have known what to do with it. Chuck it in the garbage?

Keep it for all time? It's not like I have a collection of baby teeth. Especially not little-brother ones with itty-bitty specks of dried blood on them.

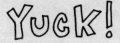

Anyway, Matt is smiling as wide as can be. I must admit, he looks pretty cute with that gap where his tooth used to be.

I wish he hadn't woken us up so so so early, but for him it must feel like Christmas morning. He said he thinks the tooth fairy gave him more than one kind of money because his tooth was loose in more than one country.

Mom and Dad are still fast asleep in their room, so Cecily and I told Matt to go back to sleep too. He said he'd try. But first he danced twice around the room with DogDog. He says DogDog won't stop licking him!

Good night and good morning!

MelBelle the Hero

P.S.

WHen Matt the Brat lost his tooth,
I had a big moment of truth.
So when we get back to New York,
I might stop calling him a dork.

(But don't count on it—hee hee!)

Same morning, but a more
normal hour

Dear Diary,

Mom tiptoed in while Cecily and Matt were still asleep. I waved, and she looked right at me, and then Matt, and she blew me *een*, *twee*, *drie* kisses. I whispered that I wanted to ask her something. We went into her room and Dad was shaking a tower, so I snuggled into bed with Mom. She said she loved me and that's when I asked, "How do you *know* you're healthy?"

"I know because I get regular check-ups called mammograms."

"So you promise you're okay?"

"Pumpkin, I take good care of myself. But that's not

the kind of thing anyone can promise because life does not come with guarantees."

I wish it did.

TVs do.

I'm glad I was able to ask her, though.

Anne Frank wasn't able to ask her mom personal questions. She and her mom did not get along well. She and her dad did. And Anne hoped that someday she'd be a good "mumsie" herself.

Today we're going to Anne Frank's house. It is now a museum called the *Anne Frank Huis* (Anna Frahnk House). I've read some more of her diary—by myself and with Mom. So far, Anne has been cooped up for *over a year and a half.* She wrote that when she looks out the window, all she sees are raincoats and hats and the tops of people's umbrellas. And that she misses good food and new books and the smell of fresh air. And that she feels like a "songbird whose wings have been clipped."

Reading her diary makes me feel guilty for ever saying I was bored and for not always appreciating my plain old regular life. Just yesterday, I signed off,

"Melanie, A Culture Vulture with Tired Wings." But think about it: Tired wings are no fun, but clipped wings are so much worse!

I have decided never to complain or feel sorry for myself again for the rest of my life.

Appreciatively yours,
Melanie

late morning

Dear Diary,

Breakfast today was disgusting! We went downstairs and they ran out of cereal, so there was just grainy bread and gross cheese and gooshy yogurt.

Even the Dutch word for breakfast is stupid. It's *ontbijt* (Ont Baid). Lunch is spelled *lunch* (Lunch) and dinner is *diner* (Dee Nay). But *ontbijt*! What kind of a dumb word is—

Oops.

I forgot about not complaining.

Anne Frank once got a bottle of yogurt as a holiday present and considered it a big deal.

I *am* trying to be a better person. But it doesn't happen overnight (or overmorning).

TRYING trying trying,
Mellie

P.S. If I do have a little badness inside me, I wonder if there's a way to get rid of it so it doesn't grow back.

lunchtime

Dear Diary,

At the Anne Frank house we were waiting on a line that crossed the street. Since I was reading her diary, I sort of had my nose in a book. Suddenly, Mom pushed me toward the curb because a car was zooming in my direction. As the car was driving away from us, Mom pounded on the back of it with her fist.

Guess what?

The car *stopped*! The driver got out! He marched over to Mom and shouted in English, "What were you doing?"

"What were *you* doing?" Mom said.

"You hit my car!" the man said.

"You almost hit my daughter!" Mom said. "You need to slow down."

"Don't hit my car again or you'll be swimming in the canal!" the man said.

I thought Mom should leave it at that. But she said, "Don't you drive into a line of people as though they were bowling pins!"

The man cursed in Dutch (I think it was cursing and I think it was Dutch), then got back in his car and sped away.

He obviously has big chunks of badness in him.

Mom hardly ever gets that mad. I wasn't sure whether to be embarrassed or proud. I mean, her nostrils were practically flaring! You could tell that people in line were talking about us, but at least it wasn't in English.

"What a jerk," Dad said. "Maybe he's a young Nazi."

Matt said, "What's a Not See? Someone who can't see?"

"Nazi, not Not See," Mom said. "But actually, Matt, the Nazis were big bullies—thugs—who thought they were better than everybody else. They could *not see* that what they were doing was appalling—horrible. Nazis were bad guys who were killing millions of innocent people, mostly Jews, during World War II until finally America, Russia, Great Britain, and other countries beat them and won the war." Mom said we'd study this later in school. She also reminded me that Anne Frank called them "the cruelest brutes that walk the earth."

Cecily said that she and her dad recently went to the Holocaust Memorial Museum in Washington. "There was a whole wall of drawings by kids," she said. "Some were cute and made you smile, and some were of scary things and made you sad; but it was all just kid art, like the stuff we do." She looked at Matt and me. "Only all those sketches were probably the last ones those kids *ever* got to do because they were Jewish and they got killed."

"I don't get it," Matt said. "What's wrong with being Jewish?"

"Nothing!" Cecily said. "It was Hitler who was wrong. He was a high school dropout who became a dictator. And he was worse than any bad guy on TV or in comics or video games or computer games or anything. He was maybe the meanest person who ever lived! He was the *opposite* of tolerant. He wanted everyone to be the same. But a lot of people listened to him—maybe some were afraid not to—and so millions of people got killed. Jews and gays and gypsies and disabled people—he picked on all kinds of people. And by 'picked on,'" Cecily said, "what I really mean is *mass murdered*."

Matt didn't say a word. Me neither.

I had no idea that Cecily knew all that stuff. But maybe some people are like some paintings—the more you look, the more you see.

I'm beginning to realize that friends don't have to be peas in a pod anyway. Friends can be a bunch of different vegetables mixed up in a *hutspot*!

Well, the line kept moving forward and we finally got inside, and we climbed lots of stairs and reached the famous hinged bookcase that blocked the doorway. Behind it, more stairs lead to the "Secret Annex" where Anne and the others lived. Anne had written, "No one would ever guess that there would be so many rooms hidden behind that plain gray door." (For a long time, no one did.)

We got to see all four rooms, the bathroom, and the attic where all eight people (the two families and the grumpy man) were squeezed in and where they had to stay totally quiet even when they were fighting or cooking or taking sponge baths.

I could almost picture Anne writing in her diary in the different rooms, trying to keep her spirits up even though she was desperate to, as she put it, have "some rollicking fun."

I say "almost picture" because the truth is, it was hard to really truly feel Anne there. You know how when you tour a famous person's home, a guide points out the frilly canopy bed and antique grandfather clock and dining room table set for tea? Well, there was no guide or fancy furniture. But on the wall, Anne had hung pictures of movie stars cut out from magazines, and it reminded me of Cecily's celebrities. Which felt sort of eerie. And sad.

We took ourselves up to the attic and looked out the window at the clock tower, the Westertoren

(Vester Tour N). I remembered how Anne's family couldn't get used to the clock chiming every quarter hour, but how Anne said she loved the sound, even at night, because it was like "a faithful friend." She really needed a faithful friend!

We walked back down and got to see Anne's actual red-and-white-plaid diary (behind glass). That was amazing! I tried again to picture Anne writing and writing, and maybe wondering if her story would have a happy ending.

We also saw dozens of translations of her diary, each with a different cover. And we watched some short films.

I think deep down Anne *knew* she was a good writer and that other people would read her diary someday. But I don't think she knew that her work (like van Gogh's and Vermeer's) would really be appreciated only after her death. She certainly did not know what would happen to her.

What happened to her is what happened to a lot of people. The German police raided the annex and found her and the others and rounded them up and sent them to concentration camps, where guards were cruel and there wasn't enough food and people got sick and were exterminated as though they were bugs.

Anne and her mother and sister all died.

Anne was only fifteen.

Somehow her father survived, and after the war, he returned to Amsterdam. His friends had found Anne's diary and they handed it to him. He read it (that must have been so sad) and decided to turn it into a book. He wanted the diary to help other children and grown-ups understand what had gone on so it would never happen again.

I bet he also wanted the diary to help keep Anne alive forever.

Which it sort of has.

Humbly yours,
Melanie

P.S. I asked if the father was still alive, and Mom said that he died in 1980 at age 91. Matt asked if Hitler got thrown in jail. Dad said he ended up killing himself after

193

he realized he lost the war. "And you know what else, Matt?" Cecily said. "No one names their son Adolf anymore and no one wears that stupid little mustache anymore either. And now when someone acts horrible, the rest of the world usually pays attention sooner and tries to stop him."

afternoon
in line for a canal-boat ride

Dear Diary,

We were finishing lunch at a café on a tree-lined canal, and Matt said that we were taking too long and if we'd gone to McDonald's, we'd be done by now. Dad said, "We don't want to be done. We're on vacation." Mom told him to listen to the church tower bells—the carillon—and to appreciate the moment.

I love how the church bells ring out melodies. I wish bells did that in our neighborhood.

I also wish it were not our last day in Holland even though I know Cecily is ready to see her parents.

Well, Dad started going on about some "brilliant"

194

Dutch writer named Erasmus, and all of us kids started dying of boredom. Cecily and I looked at each other. "Not to change the subject," I said, "but can we take a canal-boat ride?"

At the exact same time, Mom and Dad said, "Sure."

Then Mom smiled at us and shouted, "Jinx!" We all cracked up because Dad didn't even know that you're supposed to say "Jinx!" when you and someone else say the same thing.

Every kid knows that it stinks
To be the last one shouting, "JINX!"

In Line (not online)
MEL

bedtime

Dear Diary,

Our canal-boat guide's name was Hanneke (pronounced like Hah Nuh Kuh—the Jewish holiday Hanukkah). She spoke lots of different languages and pointed out skinny houses with cool stairstep roofs, old bridges, houseboats, the mayor's home, and all the twinkly lights of the city at twilight. She even pointed out five ducks swimming along beside us.

It was all so pretty, it felt like a movie!

Back at the canal house, we got dressed up, and polished each other's nails, then went to a fancy restaurant with chandeliers called Café Américain. The waiter was really nice and he said, *"Eet smakelijk"* (Ate Smock Ay Lick), which we all know means "Enjoy your food."

We talked about what we liked best here in Holland. Mom said the art museums. Dad said the topless beach (but then he said he was kidding—he liked Haarlem). Matt said the wax museum and his chocolate-sprinkle sandwich. I said the buggy ride. Cecily said she liked the whole entire trip.

We also talked about what we wish we could have seen. Mom said more museums (so we made fun of her). Dad said the Heineken brewery (so we made fun of him). Matt said the zoo. I said Madurodam, which is a mini-city with scale models of Dutch windmills and castles and bridges and boats. Cecily said she liked the trip exactly the way it was.

I don't think she was just trying to be a family pet,

though. I think she has a mostly good attitude.

I also think Cecily and I both liked the getting-along part of the trip more than the fighting part.

Dessert was pudding and *appeltaart* (Ah Pull Tahrt) or apple tart. In the middle, Cecily handed Mom and Dad the present that had been in her lost luggage. It was a beautiful silver frame. Mom oohed and aahed and Dad said they would put a vacation photo of all of us in it.

It was nice of Cecily to give my parents a thank-you gift.

Would it be nice of me to give her mom a get-well gift???

At the end of dinner, a man from the next table came over. I was sure he was going to say we had been loud or bad-mannered, but he said, "Such charming children! And so well-behaved!"

Mom thanked him and it was as though we agreed by mind reading that we would *not* tell the man that we are not always thaaaat well-behaved—hee hee.

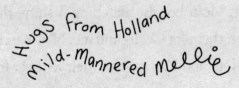

Hugs from Holland
Mild-Mannered Mellie

August 19

afternoon at **Ski Pole** Airport

Dear Diary,

We packed up, and while Mom and Dad made sure we had everything, Matt, Cecily, and I played Window Spy. Matt looked out the window and described what he saw down below, and Cecily and I both drew the boats and people and bicycles. It was fun and it did *not* feel like a competition.

We're now about to fly to London and then New York, and this time, trust me, I packed Hedgehog in my backpack. I also packed Melanie Martin's diary (you!) for writing and Anne Frank's diary for reading.

Anne is thinking about her old boyfriends and the older boy, Peter, who is stuck with her in the Secret Annex. She's also thinking about how she's growing inside and outside. She says growing up is "so wonderful."

I think I am growing more inside than outside. But who knows? Maybe I'm growing everywhere.

At the airport, Mom bought matching T-shirts that say AMSTERDAM on them for Cecily and me. Now we can be twins! Then Mom and Dad gave us their leftover for-

198

eign coins and said we could buy whatever we wanted. Matt spent his coins—and his tooth-fairy money—on candy. Dad said the tooth-fairy would approve because candy will help make Matt's other teeth fall out. But Dad bought Dutch candy too—black licorice that is *way* too salty.

Cecily and I spent our money on postcards and Droste chocolate and Dutch red and white and blue flags.

I also wanted to buy something for Mrs. Hausner. But what? I looked at tulip coasters and Delft tiles and bulb bags. Then I saw two little Dutch clogs. Matt said, "I wouldn't choose wooden shoes. Try it, Mel! It's a tongue twister!"

I said, "I wouldn't choose wooden shoes, I wouldn't choose wooden shoes, I wouldn't choose wooden shoes. It's not that hard."

But I chose a pair anyway. They were made of china, not wood. They were white with blue windmills on them and they hang on a red string.

Mom said they were charming. "They look like they could be a Christmas ornament."

Dad said that in Holland, Santa comes way early—on December 5, on the night before his birthday. "Instead of coming by reindeer from the North Pole, he comes by ship from Spain, then travels on his white horse. And instead of filling stockings, he and his faithful servant, Pete, fill shoes." So kids put their shoes by the fireplace and put carrots and straw in them for the horse. Then, when Santa and Pete reach the rooftop, Pete slides down the chimney and replaces the shoe carrots with candy, chocolate letters, and little presents. Dad said that the name Santa Claus comes from the Dutch *Sinterklaas* (Sin Tear Class), which comes from Saint Nicholas, who was really a Turkish bishop who was nice to poor kids.

Personally, I feel kind of like Santa Claus myself—like Melanie the Grinch is becoming Melanie the Generous.

Ho Ho Ho,
Melanie Martin,
NEW AND IMPROVED

Dear Diary,

The flight to London was short and smooth, and now we're flying the rest of the way home. The airline people announced, "This is your final boarding opportunity," which Dad said meant "Get on the plane N-O-W or we'll take off without you." So we got on and sat down.

I like how planes can be like flying libraries. I've almost filled up this new diary, and guess what? Dad, who never buys me anything except on birthdays or Christmas, bought me a present. In Heathrow Airport, he bought me another diary. He said that he admires how I'm always writing (especially on trips) and that I can use it for my next adventure.

Dank u wel, Dad!

In Anne Frank's diary, I'm up to the part where Anne is in love with Peter. One minute she's all upset and the next she's all happy. It depends on if she and Peter get to talk. "Who would ever think that so much can go on in the soul of a young girl?" Anne asks.

Answer: I would!

I mean, I've never had a boyfriend or anything, but even just talking—or not talking—to Cecily can make me feel up or down.

still on board

Speaking of ups and downs, planes have them too, and I'm glad we're going to land soon. But I'm doing a good job of staying calm (yay me!) even though there's nothing under us except wide open ocean.

Matt just said, "Why do seagulls fly over the sea?"

I said, "I give up. Why?"

Matt said, "Because if they flew over the bay, they'd be *bay*-gulls! Get it?"

Cecily and I laughed and we all agreed that we miss bagels.

Almost home,

MANHATTAN MEL

home in my nice soft bed 🛏️

Dear Diary,

I like being home.

Amsterdam the city is over 3,500 miles away.

Amsterdam *Avenue* is two blocks away.

Mom and Dad have been busy unpacking and doing laundry and reading e-mail and snail mail, so they are letting Matt and me watch a ton of TV. And we are. We are making up for lost time. The only problem is that the commercials keep talking about back-to-school sales.

Isn't that obnoxious? They're rubbing it in!

Sometimes I wish that along with summer vacation, we also had long long long fall, winter, and spring vacations.

Then I could get more and more stamps on my passport!

C-Ya

BACK-TO-SCHOOL MEL

P.S. Cecily called and thanked my parents again and told us the good news that her mom is feeling much better.

early morning in the kitchen

Dear Diary,

Because of jet lag, we've been going to bed early and waking up early.

Well, yesterday, Mom was reading me Anne Frank's diary, and I asked if she ever reads *my* diary. She said no because that would be an invasion of privacy. Then she told me that a fun thing about art is that it *lets* you invade people's privacy. For instance, Vermeer (the guy who painted *The Milkmaid*) painted lots of ladies reading or writing love letters, which obviously was their personal business. But since the ladies are in paintings, not real life, you're *allowed* to peek all you want.

"The women think they're alone, but they're not," Mom said. "They're being watched—by us! Vermeer invites us to snoop!" She even told me that the word "snoop" comes from Dutch.

Anyway, in Anne Frank's private diary, she is now fourteen, almost fifteen, and Peter, the boy in hiding with her, just kissed her! The first time he kissed her, it was sort of half on her ear and half on her cheek and right through her hair. But later, he kisses her on the lips! And she kisses back!

They have now spent two whole years in hiding. Poor Anne is getting bored and hungry. All they usually have to eat is porridge, stale bread, rotten potatoes, beans, sauerkraut, and spinach. (And I was complaining about fondu!) But she keeps writing and reading and she says, "I love Holland," and she says she loves the Dutch and it's a glorious spring and the chestnut tree outside is in full bloom. It's really incredible how she stayed calm and cheerful when she had every reason not to be.

We also read a part where Anne hopes she'll be an author someday. Anne wrote, "I want to go on living even after my death! And therefore I am grateful to God for giving me this gift, this possibility of developing myself and of writing, of expressing all that is in me."

Suddenly Mom's voice got wobbly and her eyes got shiny.

"What's wrong?" I said.

"It's just so poignant," Mom said.

"What's *poignant?*"

"Sad, bittersweet, touching."

"*What* is?" I asked. I wondered if that was a stupid question. Or an insensitive one?

"Oh sweet pea, it just makes me sad to think of this lonely, hard-working, talented girl. She was just a few years older than you—the age of my students. And she was an optimist, and a self-improver, full of hope and ambition and even gratitude!"

Mom's voice was still wobbling, so I added, "She should have had her whole life ahead of her."

Mom reread the line where Anne wrote that her "greatest wish" is to become a journalist and "a famous writer." Anne even wrote that she wanted to publish a book about living in the Secret Annex!

It almost makes you feel a little better about snooping into her diary because she wanted to share her work and because she *did* become a famous writer. She became the most famous girl writer in the world.

But it also makes you feel so much worse because Anne Frank could have written lots of books and lived lots of years—and maybe even become a "mumsie."

She was just getting started.

Privately Yours,
Melanie

afternoon on the living room sofa

Dear Diary,

We just finished Anne Frank's diary.

We read where she wrote, "We're going to be hungry, but anything is better than being discovered." And, "In spite of everything I still believe that people are really good at heart."

I don't know if Anne was ever an ordinary kid, but I know she was an extraordinary teenager.

Mom was reading me an entry about how there are two Annes: an inside one and an outside one, a cheerful one and a deeper one, a bad one and a good one. Then Mom stopped reading.

"That's it?" I said.

"That's it," Mom said. The diary ends in the middle because the Gestapo—Nazi police—burst in on them and sent them away to concentration camps, where they all died except the father.

Even though I already *knew* that Anne never got to turn sixteen, the end of the book still came as sort of a shock. I just sat there all heavy and numb.

Dad came in and sat down with us. "You finished the book?"

"It ends in the middle," I said. "It should have ended with 'Hurray! The war is over and now I'm going back to school. Yours, Anne.'"

"She almost made it," Dad said. "The Americans and British landed in France on June 6, 1944, and the war was over within the year. But that was the summer the Franks were arrested. Anne died of a disease called typhus in the concentration camp the next spring."

"What about the friends, the ones who helped hide them and who found the diary?" I asked. "Did they get in trouble?"

Dad said that they were punished but not killed.

"They were heroes too, just like the soldiers," Mom said. "And like firefighters, and the police, and all the people who risk their lives to protect others."

Dad said there's an Anne Frank Center downtown and it teaches children about Anne Frank, tolerance, and "the dangers of discrimination."

Well, I will tell you one thing: I can't stop thinking about Anne Frank. Normally I get a song from the radio stuck in my head, but now I have Anne Frank stuck in my head.

Usually when I finish a book I like, I feel proud of myself but also sort of sad that the book is over. In this case, I feel sad because Anne Frank's *life* was over. She didn't get to grow up.

When the Nazis started taking over Germany, Anne's family went to Holland. When the Nazis took over Holland, they went into hiding. And when the Nazis raided their Secret Annex, they went to concentration camps. They couldn't just stay put and feel safe and live their lives!

And millions of perfectly nice people got treated like this. Anne was just one.

How could this have happened? How could grown-ups kill each other and let kids die??

I guess sometimes just feeling safe is a luxury.

And just being kind or helpful makes a difference.

Would I risk my life to help my friends if they needed me? I think I would. (But I'd probably whine about it.)

I hope I can stay aware of what's important and what's not.

Right now, this very second, I feel like I "get it." And I'm going to keep trying to see the Big Picture and be a Better Person.

But don't expect me to have an instant personality transplant or anything. I *am* still a kid!

Yours,
Mel

5:30 P.M.

Dear Diary,

I just wrote a poem for Mom. It's sort of dumb but it's the kind of thing she'll appreciate.

I've thought about it and I can't
Let you think I hate Rembrandt.
I was just trying to disagree
With everything said by Cecily.
So I'll admit (since we're over our fight)
That for an Old Master, Rembrandt's all right.

Better late than never,
Mel

210

bedtime

Dear Diary,

Mom liked my poem and showed me some Rembrandt self-portraits. He looked wise and kind. Mom said "soulful." Mom also showed me a Vermeer book that shows cool close-ups of his signatures. Sometimes he combined the V and M of Vermeer, like this:

VMeer

Yours,

Melanie
Martin

August 25
afternoon on my floor

Dear Diary,

Matt declared today W.B. Day for Walking Backwards Day. He's been walking around the house backwards for the last two hours. He even walked into my room backwards and said, "Ttam si eman ym."

"Is that Dutch?" I said.

"It's 'My name is Matt' backwards. You can call me Ttam."

I rolled my eyes and didn't call him anything.

He started dealing cards.

"What are you playing?" I asked.

"Raw," he said.

"Raw?"

"Raw."

"War?!"

He nodded.

"By yourself?" I asked.

He nodded again.

"That's pathetic," I said.

"Do you want to play Rj Eulc?"

"What's Rj Eulc?" I said.

"Clue Jr.," he said.

I was going to say "You need mental help," but instead, I decided to make his day and said, "Erus."

I didn't even add "Tarb eht Ttam."

EVOL,

Einalem

Dear Diary,

Matt was still walking backwards after dinner and he banged into Dad's reading lamp and knocked it over. It didn't break but Dad got really mad and said, "How can we learn from this?" (Hee hee.)

By the way, did I ever tell you that thanks to me, four kids in my class now have made-up names for their brothers or sisters? It's true: Will the Pill, Nicky the Picky, Burke the Jerk, and Elaine the Pain. I'm an inspiration!

Inspiringly yours,

Mel

P.S. There's one thing I still have to do before school starts: VISIT MRS. HAUSNER!

August 28
afternoon in the living room

Dear Diary,

I *still* haven't given Mrs. Hausner her present.

213

I am such a chicken!! Bok bok bok.

I was thinking maybe I could just write her a note apologizing for hanging up on her. Or scribble something like "Dear Mrs. Hausner, Get well soon. This is for you. Melanie."

Deep down, though, I *know* I should go see her in person. I've known her forever and she went through this terrible thing and I've been acting like I don't even know about it.

Gotta run. Cecily is coming for a sleepover.

L8R,
Melanie the Procrastinator

Dear Diary,

Breakfast was French toast, which Matt calls French toes, which cracked Cecily up. Mom got the maple syrup from the cupboard instead of the refrigerator (where it belongs). Since she had opened it a few days ago, Matt kept asking, "Are you sure nothing fuzzy is growing on it?" and Mom kept saying, "Enough, Matt! I'm sure."

Then Mom announced that school starts next week.

The weird thing is that I don't think any of us minds that much. Matt is excited about second grade, and Mom is excited about the assemblies she is giving on van Gogh, and Cecily never minds school (maybe because things are usually pretty quiet at her home).

And me? Just between us, I'm almost looking forward to school starting up again.

I realize that if I were in hiding, I would miss not just marshmallows and M&M's and pretzel goldfish and slice 'n' bake cookie dough and Chinese food. I would miss school. And my friends. And the whole wide world.

Anne did.

We showed Cecily the frame she gave us, which now has a photo of us all in Holland. It's the cheesy picture taken by Hans. I can hardly believe I was practically competing with Cecily over him when obviously best friends matter more than cute tour guides.

afternoon in the Kitchen

Dear Diary,

I did it. I talked to Mrs. Hausner.

Matt and I were playing archeologist with chocolate-chip cookies and toothpicks and paintbrushes. The game is Dig the Dinosaur Eggs out of Their Nests, and the object is to get the chips out whole—without breaking or eating them. I always win because Matt can never resist snacking on his chocolate dino eggs.

Well, I knew I couldn't just keep playing games and being a bok-bok chicken. So I called Cecily—even though she's at her father's. Part of me was hoping to get her answering machine, but I got her mom.

"Hello, Mrs. Hausner, this is Melanie," I said. Then, instead of saying, "May I please speak to Cecily?" I said, "How are *you*?"

"Fine, thank you," Mrs. Hausner said, "But Cecily's at her father's. She won't be home until tomorrow."

"I know. I was calling to talk to you." Mrs. Hausner probably thought she'd heard wrong because she didn't say a word. "Could I drop something off?" I asked.

"Sure, unless you'd rather give it to Cecily when she gets back."

"It's not for Cecily—it's for you." I started thinking that it might be fun to surprise Cecily with a gift someday too. Maybe a little bag of FAO Schwarz M&M's— regular blue, light blue, and dark blue.

Next thing you know, the Dutch shoes were in my pocket, and I asked Mom to walk me over to Mrs. Hausner's. Mom was doing a puzzle of her favorite Vermeer painting: *Girl with a Pearl Earring*. It's in Holland but not in Amsterdam, so we didn't get to see it. It's really really beautiful, and when you look at it, sometimes you see a girl, and other times you see a young woman.

Well, Mom and I walked outside and I told her everything. Everything! About the manners lessons and messy kitchen and even hanging up on Mrs. Hausner. (I said I did it "a couple times," not *three* times.) Then I asked Mom if she'd ever done anything like that. She said, "Mellie, it's not something I'm proud of, but yes, when I was in grade school, my best friend and I made a few phony phone calls. That was before the days of Caller I.D.!" (Ha! Even Mom was not a perfect kid.)

Mom wished me good luck and said she'd pick me up ten minutes later.

I rang the Hausners' doorbell. Instead of a *ding-dong*, it has a melody. Like a carillon.

In the middle of the melody (middle of the melody—is that a tongue twister?), Mrs. Hausner answered. She looked the *exact same* as ever. She said, "Come in! Tell me about Holland. And thank you for being such a wonderful friend to Cecily. She had a terrific time."

I was taking off my sandals and Cheshire Cat rubbed up against me and started purring like a motor. I petted him, got up my nerve, and stood up.

"We all had a good time, but I came to say that I'm sorry about when I kept hanging up on you. Also, I really hope you're feeling better."

Mrs. Hausner seemed surprised. She looked at me in a proud-mother sort of way, and said, "Melanie, you're a good egg."

I didn't know what that was supposed to mean, but I figured being a good egg had to be better than being a bad chicken.

I handed her the present. "This is for you, Mrs. Hausner."

"Oh, how sweet!" she said, then added, "Now that you're getting older, you may call me Priscilla."

"I'll try," I said, which was sort of stupid because how hard can it be to call someone Priscilla? It's not like it's tricky to pronounce. Still, she's always been Mrs. Hausner to me, so I wasn't positive I could just *een*, *twee*, *drie* make the switch.

Mrs. Priscilla opened the gift. "These are lovely!"

"I know you don't allow shoes inside your home, but I hope you'll make a special exception."

"I know just where to put them!" She thumbtacked them on their bulletin board.

They looked pretty cute up there if I do say so myself. And having my shoes in her kitchen made me feel like I'm sort of part of Cecily's family—just as Cecily is sort of part of mine.

219

"Thank you," she said, and hugged me. Her chest felt the same as always (not that I was paying attention).

"You're welcome." I would have added "Priscilla," but I'm going to have to practice saying "Priscilla Priscilla Priscilla" by myself before I can say it out loud in public. I don't think it's going to come popping out on its own.

L and K,
Melanie (but you can call me Mellie)

August 30
almost bedtime

Dear Diary,

Cecily got home, and we went bowling, and I got my first strike ever!

We each paid our own way. That's called going Dutch.

When two people go Dutch,
Neither one pays too much.

Dad said the Dutch have a reputation for being careful with their money. If two people go out for dinner, a Dutch person might say "Let's split the bill," or "Let's go half and half," rather than "It's on me," or "My treat."

Then again, a Dutch person might not say any of those things. When you're sensitive, you realize you can never just assume stuff about other people.

Personally, I think going Dutch is good because everyone does their part.

Double Dutch is good too. That's the jump-rope game when two girls turn two ropes at a time, and if you're the jumper, you have to jump like crazy and really pay attention to what everyone else is doing.

Mom finished her Vermeer puzzle, then sighed this big loud sigh. I think she knows summer is about to be over.

I'm excited about school and seeing friends. But I'm a little nervous too. In fifth grade, I doubt we'll have D.E.A.R. time (Drop Everything and Read). And I doubt we'll get to wear slippers on Winter Wednesdays (I love coming in from the frozen playground and putting on my slippers). And I don't even know if we'll get to bring cupcakes to school. I hope so!

I *do* know that we'll start learning a foreign language. I picked Spanish.

¡Adiós!

Melanie

August 31

afternoon

Dear Diary,

Cecily and I came up with the best idea! We were baking a double batch of chocolate-chip cookies in my kitchen (fairly neatly, if I do say so myself) and we decided to have a bake sale. But instead of keeping the money, we decided to give it to the place Dad said teaches kids about tolerance.

We made a sign that said, "Cookies 25 Cents! All Money Goes to the Anne Frank Center USA."

At first it was embarrassing sitting with Cecily and our sign and our cookie tray on a blanket on the sidewalk next to my doorman Benny. But then my neighbors started stopping by—including some I hardly ever see except on Halloween. Almost everybody was really friendly. Some asked where we got the idea, and some handed us a dollar for just one or two cookies and wouldn't take any change back. Even a few *strangers* stopped by.

One old lady with short gray hair and a sweet face gave us TEN DOLLARS FOR ONE COOKIE! She said she escaped from Germany during World War II when she was a young teenager, and that we were "wonderful wonderful girls." She even shook our hands, mine and Cecily's. Her hand was small and soft and ghosty, and I shook it very gently.

After she walked away, Cecily whispered, "Anne Frank would have been around her age!"

"Really?" I said.

"Yes, she was born in 1929, remember?"

I didn't remember but I did do the math in my head. Cecily was right: if Anne Frank had lived and become a "mumsie," she might have become a grandmother too. Maybe a nice one with a nice laugh—and nice grandkids.

Well, we were down to the last cookie, so we offered it to Benny for free, but he gave us a dollar and told us to donate the change. (He is sooo nice.) Then we started sorting out coins, smoothing out bills, and counting it all up.

Guess how much we raised?? Seventy-eight dollars!!!

We *did* feel like wonderful wonderful girls!

We might even do another sale someday. Maybe for breast cancer research or Children's Aid or the Red Cross. Or maybe just for our own selves, though to tell you the truth, it felt good to make money for an important cause.

IMPORTANTLY,
MELANIE THE FUNDRAISER

Dear Diary,

I gave Dad the pile of money, and instead of grumbling about the nickels, dimes, quarters, and crinkly bills, he said, "Good for you, cupcake," and wrote out a check. I mailed it with a note from Cecily and me.

After dinner, the phone rang, and Mom got on, talked for a while, then handed it over saying, "It's for you. It's Priscilla."

For some reason, my heart started pounding. Why would Mrs. Hausner call *me*? What did I do wrong *now*? I looked at Mom for a clue, but she just shrugged.

"Hi, Priscilla," I said. The "Priscilla" part came out a little forced.

"Hi, Melanie. I'm so proud of you and Cecily!" she said. "If you want to have another bake sale, I hope you'll come bake over here." I didn't know what to say. I wished she could have seen that I was nodding at least.

I said, "Okay, Priscilla, it's a deal," and then she put Cecily on the phone.

Love,

Melanie,
Cookie Baker and Deal Maker

P.S. Just in case I ever forget it, I'm taping in my recipe for Ten-Dollar Cookies:

In a bowl, mix two sticks of butter with 3/4 cups of sugar. Add two eggs (cracked) and a teaspoon of vanilla. Stir. Add 2 1/4 cups of flour. Stir. Add a big bag of chocolate chips. Stir. Drop the cookie dough in blobs onto ungreased cookie sheets, and bake (but don't burn) them in a preheated 375 degree oven for around seven minutes or until they are more golden than gushy.

EAT'EM OR SELL'EM !

→ Labor Day morning

Dear Diary,

I almost forgot about the labor (get it?) I'm supposed to do: the what-I-read-and-what-I-learned book report. I was about to PANIC when I remembered it has to be only a hundred words.

I think the teachers just want to be sure we don't forget how to read. It would be bad if we all started fifth grade sounding out words.

Over spring break, I had to write a thirty-line poem

226

for school, and I practically had a heart attack over it. But I got it done. Now since I am more mature, I realize I *can* write and I *can* count so I *can* do this.

I've decided to do my report on the diary of Anne Frank.

Wish me luck!

Motivated Mellie

P.S. When I finish, I'll copy it in here.

Labor Afternoon

Dear Diary,

Dad once said that the most important part of writing is rewriting. He told me Isaac Bashevis Singer, who won the Nobel Prize for writers (which is like the Academy Award for actors) said, "The wastepaper basket is a writer's best friend."

Well, my wastepaper basket is full of crumpled-up sentences. Perfectly good ones, too. I admit that I spent a long time on a short report, but this is the first assignment of the year, and I wanted to make a good impression.

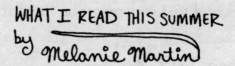

WHAT I READ THIS SUMMER
by Melanie Martin

This summer I read The Diary of a Young Girl by Anne Frank. Anne was an excellent person who lived in a terrible time. Anyone who reads her diary will be different afterward. It makes you ask: How could someone be so evil that he would stop a kid from growing up? How could other people let him?

Of course, not everybody sat back. Some people did try to stop Hitler and to help. They were heroes. They really really understood that being a good person cannot just mean doing nothing wrong. It also has to mean doing something right.

Sincerely,

Melanie

P.S. I probably shouldn't have written "really really" but I really really needed two more words.

Dear Diary,

Well, even though I finished my book report, here I am back at my desk. A poem was rumbling around in my head, so I figured I might as well let it out.

It's actually pretty cheesy—but you know what? I'm blaming that on Holland!

Besides, who cares? It's not for school. It's for my 👀 only.

Remember my fortune cookie?
Well, I went back and took a lookie.
It hinted that my Dutch vacation
Might lead to great transSformation

I always liked myself before,
But now I have walked through a door,
And I have learned that to be wise
You have to open up your eyes,
And try on other points of view,
And maybe make a change or two.

We're all living out our days
In lucky or less lucky ways,
But if we seek, we'll always find
Big or small ways to be kind.

Kindly yours,

One of a Kind MELANIE

Dear Diary,

I can't believe school starts TOMORROW . Getting up early is going to make me jet-lagged all over again.

I put out my new clothes and put my book report in my new backpack. Mom and I went on a shopping spree because I'd outgrown most of my old stuff.

Mom said I'm having a "growth spurt." I don't like to think of it as a spurt. I like to think of it as growing up, inside and out.

A few minutes ago, when Mom tucked me in, I told her, "I like growing up."

"I like watching you grow up," she said.

"Do you like being already grown-up?"

"Yes."

"Why?"

"Well, you have Hedgehog, but I have you," Mom said, and kissed me on the tip of my nose.

"I love Hedgehog!" I protested. "Don't you?"

"Yes. But I love you more."

"But you *don't* love me more than Matt, and you never will, right?" I don't even know why I asked. It's like a bad habit.

"Right," Mom said. "But I'll tell you a secret."

"What?"

"I loved you first. *You* are the one who made me a mom."

I must confess, I had never thought of it that way! It's true though. Before I came along, Mom was just a regular lady. I made Mom a Mom and Dad a Dad.

That makes me . . . Mighty Melanie!

Mom kissed me good night and I started thinking

about how many Melanies I have inside me. A mighty one and a chicken one. A sweet one and a selfish one. A good one and a bad one.

And here's what I've decided: Even though I could probably be a better person, I am a pretty good person. I may have had my me-first moments, but lately I've done some good deeds. Easy ones like helping out the tooth fairy and having a bake sale, and harder ones like delivering the Priscilla present and sharing my family when Cecily needed me to.

The not-nice part of me may not be a teeny speck, but it's not a humongous chunk either. Will it ever go away completely? I doubt it. But I bet I can keep it under control.

You know what else? I'm okay with having a smidgin of not-niceness in me. After all, nobody's perfect, and I'm not *extremely* imperfect.

Dad just came in and said to turn off the light N-O-W. I told him to be tolerant and to give me one more minute. He smiled and said, "Okay, but just one."

What Dad doesn't understand is that turning off the light will be like admitting that it's the end of vacation.

Which, of course, it is.

Just like it's the end of this diary. Sigh.

Well, it definitely was *not* a bummer summer.

And now, watch out, fifth grade, here I come!

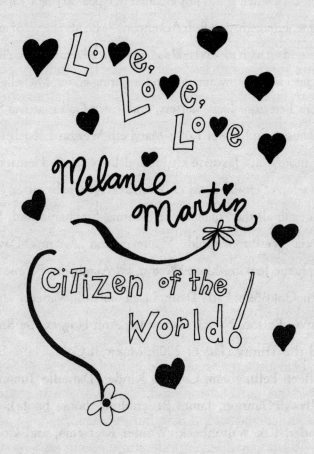

Love, Love, Love
Melanie Martin
Citizen of the World!

ACKNOWLEDGMENTS

A great big DANK U WEL to everyone who read all or part of this book back when it was just a bunch of typed-up pages. Especially Emme, Elizabeth, and Rob Ackerman—who also bicycled around Amsterdam with me and had some Martin adventures (you'll have to guess which); my amazing and inspiring editor, Michelle Frey; Laura Peterson, Joan Slattery, and Tracy Gates; artists Sarah Hokanson and Marci Roth; Marybeth Weston Lobdell (a.k.a. my mom); my favorite childhood baby-sitter, Henriette te Hasseloo of Holland; my children's favorite baby-sitter, Matty Reategui; all the Squam Lake Cousins; Stephanie Bird, M.D.; Olivia Westbrook-Gold; Maureen and Arianna Davison; Stephanie Jenkins; Mark Weston; Ed Abrahams; Bonnie Beer; Katie Goldstein; Patty Dann; Lisa Lombardi; Vanessa Wilcox; Denver Butson; Nancy Alexander; Ann Hoy, Louisa Strauss, and the Trinity class of 2008; Maxwell Coll; Claire Sabel; Colleen Fellingham; Colleen Kinder, Daneille Tumminio, Kelly McGannon, James Rosenblum (boola boola); Nick Sander, Rik Wijsenbeek, Wouter Rietsema, and Cordula Bartha (who helped with complicated pronunciations). Finally, in memory of Eric Nooter, a most noble Dutchman.